Va

Valerie Blumenthal writes numerous articles for the *Oxford Times' Limited Editions Magazine*. She runs writers groups and teaches English as a foreign language. *Knowing Me* is her fifth novel, and is a new departure for her. She has a daughter and lives with an assortment of animals in a village near Thame, Oxfordshire.

SCEPTRE

Also by Valerie Blumenthal

'To Anna', about whom Nothing is Known
The Colours of her Days
Homage to Sarah
Benjamin's Dreams

Knowing Me

VALERIE BLUMENTHAL

SCEPTRE

Copyright © 1993 Valerie Blumenthal

First published in 1995 by Hodder and Stoughton
First published in paperback in 1996 by Hodder and Stoughton
A division of Hodder Headline PLC
A Sceptre Paperback

The right of Valerie Blumenthal to be identified as the Author of the Work has been asserted by her in accordance with the Copyright, Designs and Patents Act 1988.

10 9 8 7 6 5 4 3 2 1

All rights reserved. No part of this publication may be reproduced, stored in a retrieval system or transmitted, in any form or by any means without the prior written permission of the publisher, nor be otherwise circulated in any form of binding or cover other than that in which it is published and without a similar condition being imposed on the subsequent purchaser.

All characters in this publication are fictitious and any resemblance to real persons, living or dead, is purely coincidental.

A CIP catalogue record for this book is available from the British Library

ISBN 0 340 65405 8

Typeset by Palimpsest Book Production Limited,
Polmont, Stirlingshire
Printed and bound in Great Britain by
Cox and Wyman Ltd, Reading, Berkshire

Hodder and Stoughton
A division of Hodder Headline PLC
338 Euston Road
London NW1 3BH

With thanks to my agent Merric Davidson, Dr Mark Allsopp, Consultant, Berkshire Adolescent Unit, and Ingrid Stone and Samantha Lewin for their teenage memories.

1

'I'm not sorry for what I did,' the girl says defiantly, and scratches her left nostril which has a stud pierced through it.

The man only sits with his fingertips pressed lightly together, regarding her steadily so that the girl is disquieted.

'I mean I've never got on with her. She doesn't respect me. She knows I hate my name. Everyone else calls me Gnat. Even Elliot. Daddy called me Gnat. But she? Oh no, my mother insists on calling me Natasha. "It's a lovely name, darling," she coos. She has this syrupy coo. She makes me sick. She thinks she's so great. Everyone thinks she's so great. She makes me sick.'

'What's your earliest memory?'

'My earliest memory?' The question surprises her and she considers him for a moment, her head tilted. 'You're really handsome.' And she brings her lips forward in a pout and swings her knee.

The psychiatrist stares back at her with a faint smile.

Gnat suddenly clasps her head between her hands and sways back and forth agitatedly. 'God, I don't know, I don't know. How should I know? What's the point of remembering? Get me out of here,' she shouts. 'I don't want to be stuck with a whole bunch of loony kids. Get me out, will you?'

• Valerie Blumenthal

She runs stubby, child's fingers through her multi-coloured hair. Her nails are bitten. When she looks up again her small face is pale and bland as a sleek stone.

'My earliest memory –' she speaks in a voice devoid of emotion '– is of my mother yelling at Daddy. It was night-time and I woke up. I was about three. I remember him coming into my room and cuddling me, while she went on ranting outside.'

• • •

'Natasha was three when I discovered my husband was having an affair,' the woman says, and touches the corner of her lip to hide its twitching.

'Can you list some of the principal events of your adult life?' the psychiatrist asks, disregarding her remark. Everything in time. He is elderly and there is compassion in his deeply creased forehead. Harriet is glad he isn't young. She's nervous anyway. And in pain; both kinds.

They sit opposite each other, a low table with a gleaming green plant upon it between them, and she gazes tearfully through the consulting room window, at feet walking briskly past and taxi after taxi stopping wherever they wish. He passes her a Kleenex from a box he always keeps on the table, and she takes it and turns back to the window, her angular, high cheek-boned profile to him.

'I don't understand how she could have done what she did. I don't understand what I did wrong. Where I went wrong,' she says.

And he continues to wait without offering a word or gesture of comfort. The air is gentle though, and she senses his gentleness and turns once more to him, having delved into the recesses of her memory and sifted through the kaleidescope there.

'The principal events of my adult life,' she says.

There was her first lover; her father's stroke; her marriage; the birth of her daughter; her husband's affair; her own affair; her husband's death; meeting Elliot; and now: the trauma with Natasha. Nine principal events. And in between, thousands of lesser incidents which influenced her behaviour.

Her first lover. He himself was perhaps of small consequence, but she – she had given her body and self to him and he had tossed them back at her, soiled. She was in her first year at St Martins, her idealism still intact; he had almost completed his law studies. He was disparaging about her art and her opinions and she was anxious to appeal to him. That someone of his savoir-faire had even glanced at her was astounding.

In bed, while he lay beside her smoking a cigarette, she tried to snuggle close. 'You're the first boy I've done – everything with,' she confided.

He said harshly, 'Oh come on. I cleaved through you like a knife through butter. You've been at it for years.'

The searing pain of injustice, humiliation. And the truth was she must have done it with a Tampax. She had held onto her virginity for no reason and at the end of the day with false pride: technically she had not been a virgin at all.

Thinking about it later, she was indignant: and what if she hadn't been a virgin? It was the likes of him, with his toxic blend of good looks, breeding and intellectualism, who deflowered girls with a preface of throaty endearments and the promise of expertise, then discarded them.

His scorn made a woman of her. She learned to be suspicious of men, that they lied more than women to save their own skins, and that whilst women could be bitchy, men had few scruples, a convenient conscience and were utterly selfish. She never learned that she was beautiful or to be confident about her height and thinness and small breasts, or her fine, mousey hair which she usually wore in a pony tail. She walked about with her long stride and short skirt and wide smile switching nervously on and off; and that inner light emanating from her slanting eyes so that everyone stared at her and she would wonder what they were looking at, what they had found wrong with her.

She dumped him, her first lover, before he could do it to her. Years later, when she was married and a mother, she met him in Oxford Street.

'It's strange to see you,' she said, flustered, brushing back wisps of hair, wishing she were not armed with Selfridges carrier bags, making it seem she had nothing better to do than shop all day.

'Yes. Curious,' he agreed in his old laconic manner and consulting his watch. He eyed the carrier bags and she thrust them behind her legs.

She had heard he was a successful barrister. 'How are you keeping?' she asked.

'Quite well. Thank you. I've got a big case on at the moment.' He glanced again at his watch, as though she were holding him up from it.

'That must be interesting.'

'That's one way of looking at it.'

He asked her nothing about herself. He was still handsome, with the same patronising lift of the brow, still had the same capacity for making her feel inferior. Stammering, she apologised for bothering him. And did he think of her for more than a few seconds afterwards? As she walked to the car, her cheeks burning, she remembered he had kept a day-book, filling it with incidents in his fastidious writing, and she wondered if their meeting merited an entry in it; imagined what he might write: 'Bumped into an old girlfriend today. *Quelle désastre* she looked (he'd had a habit of lapsing into affected French). Hard pushed to think of her name. Seem to remember she wasn't up to much in the sack.'

She berated herself for handling the encounter badly, hating her lack of poise, her height, her need to be liked by everyone, even now, as a mature woman. She wished she could have been forewarned about today: she would have played it so differently. She would have been regal, and he would have been awed by her, asked if he could telephone her; and she would have had the pleasure of rejecting him a second time.

She was celibate for a year after him, and discovered herself: her mind, her body, her art. The smallest thing affected her and she believed everything she was told. Her friends tried to shield her because her gullibility meant she was often disappointed. Her best friend Astrid, a girl of Swedish descent, with a broad Scandinavian face and frizzy platinum hair, was doing a course at Sotheby's. They shared a flat in London and Harriet's period of celibacy came to an end.

Her father's stroke coincided with her departure from the suburban home where she had made life more tolerable for him: God and gossip from his wife diluted with the sweet raw earnestness of his daughter, whose blossoming into a beauty he'd watched with pleasure.

The second principal event of her adult life. And her mother's voice, that smooth-nutmeg, unruffled voice, phoning her from the hospital. She was called from her life class – she can still remember the model's name – Eva, remember painting the curve of the belly in in blues and purples – and knew it could only be bad news. Her mother phoned on the dot of seven o'clock every Thursday evening to discuss the weekend's visit, never in between. Certainly not at college.

'Don't bother to come, dear. He's unconscious, so there wouldn't be much point,' she told Harriet, as though telling her not to bother buying a packet of sugar from the supermarket.

Harriet hurtled down Charing Cross Road to the station.

It was February and in her hurry she'd forgotten her coat. Her insides, her ribcage, her jaw, all of her, shook with fear and cold.

Daddy, Daddy, Daddy, was all she could think, sitting there on the scouring-pad rough seat of the tube as it flashed through darkness and light, the roughness scratching against her thin thighs, the ladders in her zig-zag patterned tights exposed where her short dark green skirt had ridden further up, paint still all over her hands.

He was in Intensive Care at the Hammersmith and apart from all the tubes connected to him, he looked normal. Pinker than usual, younger, if anything. He was fifty-five, a solicitor who dabbled at watercolour painting in his spare time. A dreamer. Her mother was there of course.

'I told you not to bother, dear,' she said when Harriet appeared like a wraith.

'I wanted to,' she said, teeth clamped against the urge to scream.

She stooped down. 'Daddy,' she whispered into his ear, watched by a sympathetic doctor who couldn't say to her, Don't worry he'll be all right.

She didn't miss a day visiting him. Timed her visits so as not to coincide with her mother. On the chair next to the bed she held his hand and reminisced with him. When his eyes opened after a few days she could pretend he understood. He was shaved, washed, smelt nice, wore a fresh nightshirt (he'd always worn a nightshirt rather than pyjamas). But he was not there with his gentle, rather pedantic advice. Since tiny childhood she'd always gone to him with her worries. They would go through them systematically and by the end he would have reassured her that they were all groundless.

The months passed. Physically he was well enough to be looked after by his wife and a nurse who came in daily. And did her mother enjoy this new power? Harriet wondered, then said guiltily to her, 'You're fantastic how you manage.'

'I took him in sickness and in health,' came the reply – which could have sounded so loving but instead sounded cryptic so that Harriet was none the wiser.

When she was nearly twenty-one she met a young doctor, and a year later they married.

The third principal event of her adult life.

Harriet falls silent and turns again to the constant stream of traffic and feet in the world beyond the window. And what of her world, irrevocably altered? It is up to this stranger, this benign-faced man, to make of it what he will, as he gently forces her to exhume the past in order to try and disentangle the present.

She blows her nose on another Kleenex.

Her husband Oliver: idealistic and strongly principled, with quietly fixed views and shadowed navy eyes that gave you their full attention. When she had first gone to bed with him and he had caressed her she had imagined his hands exploring nameless patients. Harriet, jealous of them all, of his busy, caring fingers, performed acrobatics and did everything she could think of so that he would not be bored by yet another female body. He told her to relax. He did not think of them sexually. He loved her.

He was tolerant initially with her insecurities and helped her to accept herself. While he was attached to Guys they lived in a flat in Bloomsbury and she taught art at a private school. She loved cooking for her husband – every potato, every carrot was peeled and chopped with lingering tenderness; loved being married and all the domesticity it entailed; ran to the door with a frisson of joy at the sound of his key in the lock. She liked to see their possessions all mixed together. And on the chest of drawers in their room, his hairbrush with strands of his dark hair wound amongst its bristles, flank to flank with her brush. But in the evenings he became wearier and wearier and she couldn't bear to witness his exhaustion. Then in the middle of the night the phone would ring and off he would go again, whey-faced, disenchanted and shuffling. A hundred hours or more a week, sometimes.

'It's inhuman,' Harriet protested at the end of one particular shift. 'Dangerous to the patients and inhuman to you.'

To us, to our marriage, she thought; there was nothing left of him for her.

They moved to Windsor where Harriet found another teaching job and Oliver took up the post of junior partner at a medical centre. He also held a clinic at the Royal Berkshire Hospital once a week for pregnant women. 'Fat lady day,' he cheerfully called it. He was a font of doctor jokes and anecdotes, content again now he had status and a few hours' extra sleep a week.

Plenitude. Harriet was replete with happiness. She recollects how after dinner she would sit on the floor and Oliver would lie with part of his body across her foot; as he talked she could feel his voice vibrating through her toes. When she was with him she became serene. Her restlessness was quelled. A void within her was filled. His presence reassured her and she knew he would not let her down. She would give of herself and the gift would not be tossed back, but cherished. Her father had cherished her before his stroke.

She was a child, she realises now, too dependent on another human being for the completion of her own.

'So what happened?' the psychiatrist asks in the last couple of minutes of their session.

'Natasha was born.'

• • •

Eight days. She has been here eight days. The bell's gone for tea. Lousy, lousy tea. Gnat hates how they make it here – milky and sickly. And the triangles of bread curl up in the corners, dry and hard and spread with one of those vegetable oil margerines. She only likes salted butter; lashings of it. Jason always tries to sit beside her. He makes her flesh creep with his frog-like stare and bloated cheeks. He constantly tries to touch her with damp pudgy hands, and drools at her breasts. They sprouted when she was ten, when her father was dying, and they continued to explode. She wishes they were tiny like her mother's. Not yet fourteen and these melons jutting incongruously from her slight, child's body. Harriet doesn't wear a bra.

She hates her mother. It's her fault she's in this place, she tells Dr Middleton at their session after tea, and although she hates her breasts as much as she does her mother, she sticks them out at him, as men like that.

In return he strokes his chin contemplatively.

She flops back in her chair feeling stupid and pulls her hair forward over her eyes so she can't see him. Then – tears as she recalls her dream. Her cheeks become hot and pink and wet.

'Why are you crying, Gnat?'

'I dreamed of Daddy last night. He was alive. He was hugging me. I was on his lap. And then his face became Grandpa's, all tugged down on one side and he couldn't speak to me.'

The eyes spilling sadness and the mouth opening and closing uselessly. Gnat shudders, thinking about it.

'Is Grandpa on your mother's or father's side?'

'Mother's.'

'Are you close to him?'

'How can you be close to a man who just sits there like a turnip? He had a stroke.'

'Don't you remember him before?'

'He was like it before I was born. He's very old. My mother bangs on about how he used to be. It's sad I suppose. I mean, does anything go on in his head while he just sits there? She used to make me go with her sometimes to see them. I don't go anymore. I can't stand my grandmother. Everything's God this and God that. She's like someone from a hundred years ago. She probably drove him crazy. Or maybe he's not ill at all. Maybe it's all an act so he doesn't have to speak to her. Maybe inside him he's laughing at everyone. Two fingers to them, he's thinking.'

Dr Middleton says nothing, but laces his fingers in the way with which Gnat is becoming familiar, and she picks at the stud in her nose. The silences always disconcert her. She finds herself rabbiting. Rabbit, rabbit. Once she had a pet rabbit.

'I saw some photos of Grandpa and my mother once. He was pushing her on a tricycle. In another they were on the beach together. He had his trousers rolled up. One was of her getting a prize from him at speech day. He was a school governor or something.'

A glimmer, just a glimmer passing through her mind: her mother is a girl. A girl with her own feelings and fears, who loves her father as Gnat loved hers, and sees him reduced to a turnip.

'I hate her.'

'So you said.'

Eight days. They no longer sedate her. She has stopped screaming, stopped fighting; stopped being shocked by the antics of some of the inmates; stopped disbelieving she is really here. It came to her in the night, between dreams, that nothing on earth would ever surprise or shock her again.

A weekend come and gone. Parents arriving to visit or fetch their children home. Ordinary parents with baffled expressions. The kids hang around in the recreation room pretending they're not hanging around, pretending to watch TV or read, conducting in time to their Walkmans or squabbling. But the squabbling's not in earnest. Half an ear, half an eye, is on the door, on the window, on the car pulling up outside. When the squabbling's in earnest you know it. Proper fights flaring up when a second ago everything seemed calm. Violent fights with intent to hurt. Gnat, hardened as she is from school, has never seen anything like it.

As it's summer the doors are open onto the garden. To the side is a tennis court. Apparently there had once been a pond but a boy had drowned himself and it was filled in. A terrace runs round the building and flower borders edge the lawn. For whose benefit? The second day Gnat was there someone went round and lopped off half the heads. A loony place. The garden looks onto a graveyard, and from the raised terrace white slabs are visible. Beyond, in the distance, is a wooded hill she pretends is a mountain behind the sea of gravestones, and sometimes she gazes fixedly at the suburban Surrey hill until it is transformed – and the sea is in her nostrils and ears and gulls wheel overhead. Forever ago she had walked on the beach with *her* father; and in a rubber dinghy they drifted together over choppy waves, pursued by bobbing gulls.

In her second dream last night he had been with a patient in his study, and was writing out a prescription at his desk. 'But you're dead,' she said, taking no notice of the woman with her back turned in the swivel chair. He ignored her and she tugged insistently at his sleeve. 'Do you still love me? Tell me. *Tell* me.' His arm came away from his body and he melted into a liquid mass. The woman in the chair became her mother and they were having lunch together, except the room was the dining room at Turner's End. Gnat's foot was aching and she glanced down to find it encased in dried mud. Her father was lying face-upwards on the floor and her big toe thrust through the mud into his eye. She clung to Harriet, crying out, 'I'm having an awful dream,' but didn't wake. When she did the sheet was wrapped round her left foot and the duvet was on the floor.

• Valerie Blumenthal

She lay awake for hours after, not daring to lapse back into sleep, deriving comfort from the noises of the others in the dormitory and the rims of light below and above the door. She could still feel the solid presence of her mother. In reality she had never clung to her like that.

'Gnat, I'd like you to think back to a typical weekend when your father was alive.'

She is so tired. Never has she felt such tiredness in her life. It is beginning to replace anger. Thinking makes her more tired and refills the well of sorrow within her. Her rainbow hair has faded from washing and is predominantly light brown like her mother's, but thick and curly. The roundness has gone from her cheeks. Her shoulders droop. Impossible to credit the anger, aggression and rebelliousness compacted into her body. Maria said she would make her up later. Maria is in her dormitory and has the face of a saint, of someone called Maria. She makes exquisite jewellery from shells and stones with painstaking patience. She also happens to have a split personality and is sometimes a high priestess, sometimes a whore. She is seventeen and can be violent towards herself. She doesn't know when she'll get out, where she'll go when she's too old for Turner's End adolescent home.

'My mother called me a whore once,' Gnat mused, when Maria explained about herself while serenely weaving her wheaten hair into a French plait.

A typical weekend. And her father is alive. Ordinary childhood; and in retrospect she was happy. She was ambivalent towards her mother. The shrieking episode passed quickly and dimly she recalls a period of tension about the house, her mother's aloofness, but this also passed. Her mother was beautiful and vague, issued too many orders and refused to call her Gnat.

'I'm Gnat. I want you to call me Gnat,' the little girl protested furiously.

Her father liked to tease, rarely reprimanded and helped with her homework. He took her swimming and didn't show her up by swimming like a wimp, but did a powerful crawl; and although he was quite short – shorter than Harriet – his chest was muscular with the right amount of dark hair on it. She did well at school for him, learned the cello, for him.

They lived in a rambling Edwardian house in Windsor, a five-minute walk from the river. Her mother had stripped the doors to their pine and painted murals in the dining room and one in Gnat's room.

'What was yours like?'

'It was of Pirate – our dog – chasing butterflies.'

'Did you choose it?'

'No. She just did it. I got back from school and it was there.'

'Were you pleased with it?'

'Yes. I loved Pirate. He was run over. It was dreadful.' Her voice becomes high.

'How old were you when she did the mural?'

'I don't know.' She is still thinking about the dog.

'About.'

'Seven or eight.'

'And she did it as a surprise for you?'

Gnat looks at him and says slowly, 'Yes. I really liked it.'

'Did you tell her that?'

'I don't know. How should I know? I mean it's years ago.'

'But if a person does something nice, something so caring, it's usual to show gratitude, isn't it?'

She shrugs. But she remembers the dog prancing up, and pastel butterflies and puffy clouds; remembers hugging her mother in delight.

'I hugged her,' she mutters gruffly, rubbing at her neck which feels as though a band is round it.

• Valerie Blumenthal

In the attic there was a box of old clothes, and she would dress up and put on shows; always for her father. The attic was her hideout, and he would knock before he came in. It became a joke between them.

'May I enter, Miss Edwards?'

'You may, Doctor Edwards.'

He was her best friend apart from Dimple. He never pried, but waited for her to tell him whatever she wanted. Her mother pried. Occasionally Gnat wanted to confide in her, ask her things she could not her father, but already the barrier she had constructed was too solid to demolish.

The house in Windsor is so clear: the large breakfast room with pictures she had done at school pinned to a cork board; the hall where she and Dimple searched amongst its dark panels for a sliding one that would lead them to treasure; the bathroom with the clothes horse which had to be lifted from the bath before one could climb in – and draped over the bars, her father's white pants and her mother's frilly knickers alongside Gnat's uniform grey ones.

In her room was a train set, and she and her father constructed tunnels from books; Aesop's Fables was the biggest. She was always making things, hoarded oddments and had a boxful that kept her engrossed for hours. Once she made a wire and papier-maché horse. Her father had it proudly displayed on his desk in his study, but over the years it disintegrated and for some reason started to smell fishy, and when they moved to London it crumbled to bits at the bottom of a packing case.

She can visualise the garden, and her father mowing the lawn, while Pirate kept abreast of him, barking row after row. And from within, the smells of lunch cooking, and in she would run for lick-outs and to help roll the pastry for a fruit pie.

Dimple lived up the road. Her real name was Laura, but she loathed it as much as Gnat loathed hers. When they stayed at each other's houses they had midnight feasts and related ghost stories, flicking a torch round the room and making shapes with their fingers so that dark silhouettes appeared in the halo of light on the walls. At school they were not allowed to sit next to each other because they were considered mutually distracting.

On Sundays she and Dimple and Dimple's wimpy younger brother went riding in Windsor Great Park, in an orderly stream of children on ponies – interspersed with the odd self-conscious adult on a larger horse; kicking the pony's sides, a creature stubborn as a donkey, which either bolted or bucked or refused to budge.

Sometimes they would picnic by the river, her parents and herself. She went through a phase when she insisted on wearing a favourite pair of silver party shoes and would pick her way delicately through the rough grass to avoid marking them. She remembers the excitement of unwrapping the mysterious food packages, and the newly-discovered pleasure of something as mundane as an egg-mayonnaise sandwich; and Pirate, his ears like kites, waiting for crusts. He would swim in the river, dodging boats, his head sleek, paws working like flippers, then haul himself onto the bank where he shook himself over them. And they would leap back, grabbing each other, laughing, shrieking, 'No, no.' It was all so normal then. Who would have thought she'd end up here?

One weekend, when they were wandering round the town after a picnic, she spied an owl-like creature in a souvenir shop. Tiny and bulging-eyed, made of wire and white synthetic fur, it cost fifty pence, and she was captivated by it. Her father went in to buy it.

'Better for your teeth than ice creams,' he said in his doctor's voice.

Gnat relied on her mother for ice creams.

She still has the owl. It is her mascot and she takes it

everywhere. She holds it when she goes to sleep, even though it is mostly wire, and what fur remains, matted. Her mother has posted it to her. No proper letter; just the owl and a note tied round it with a ribbon saying, love, Mummy. She threw the note away then rescued it and tucked it amongst her clothes.

She remembers a holiday in Cornwall, and walking along the quay in St Ives; dropping a pebble on the bald head of a man below to see if it would bounce. It landed in the centre of his neat Friar Tuck circle. When he reeled round she saw that he was wearing a nose shield, and she burst into laughter. He chased her, calling, 'Oi you, oi you,' as she ran to catch up with her mother.

'My daughter wouldn't do a thing like that,' Harriet defended her to him.

In private she smacked Gnat, who only said through ground-together teeth, 'Daddy never smacks me.'

Harriet burst into tears, and perhaps then, because her mother had stood by her when it mattered, Gnat felt remiss. She sought her out and offered her a fruit pastel, her favourite: a black one.

When she was about seven there was something different about her parents, and the house, too, felt different. Her mother seemed remote. And then this patch, like the other years earlier, passed, and all was harmonious again. Her mother and father were like young lovers. Jealously, Gnat watched them going out while she was left with a baby-sitter. She would part the curtains and observe them from the window, and in the glow of the street light Harriet's slanting smile was radiant.

Faint smells and sounds and sensations tug at her memory but she is unable to relate them to anything; and they flit past, leaving her wistful and seeking, bereft as a woman whose baby is stillborn. Her body is turned inside out and she wants to sleep. But dreads it. Dreads dreaming.

2

The sun streams through the window.

'Do you want me to pull the blind?' the psychiatrist asks Harriet.

'No thank you. It's lovely with the sun.'

She is more composed today, a week after their first meeting, and her pain, both kinds, is less acute. As before, she finds herself immediately engulfed by the room's atmosphere which lures words from her and unbidden thoughts.

'I was permanently tired,' she says, recalling the third year of her marriage. 'But somehow his tiredness was always more justified than mine. I don't think Oliver even recognised mine, his own was so great.'

Teaching and decorating, ironing and cooking. And up to her old acrobatics in bed because she feared Oliver was growing bored. His fingers drifted over her more casually nowadays, fiddled mechanically. His mouth lightly grazed her lips before burying itself in the pillow. Once it had latched onto hers and not let go.

She tried to appear bright, conceal her insecurity and tiredness, while he was withdrawn because of his own fatigue and his eyes were dark-ringed. What had happened to their long conversations and exchanged views? They sat sensibly on chairs instead of the floor and she tried not to be dismayed by his detachment and a certain coldness she had not suspected were part of his nature. He would frown over a newspaper, immersed in it, and her conversation died within her; she was intimidated by that excluding frown.

'What was that you said?' he would ask, peering up from the paper with a strained expression.

'Nothing,' she answered and he would immediately bury himself again.

He was unaware that she watched him sadly. He was a kind man, but disliked what he termed 'hassle'. He had enough during the day, giving continuously of himself so there was no residue. He never shouted or lost his temper. She shouted, which made him retreat – which made her more het-up. She wished she could be calm. She believed he was judging her and was afraid she'd lost his respect. She craved his praise.

With time, with familiarity, she learned to be less aggrieved by his reticence, that it was seldom directed at her or caused by her. She tried to attach less importance to things. If he doused his food with salt it wasn't because he disliked her cooking. It did not mean her body bored him because he was less demonstrative than she was, or didn't fondle her with as much enthusiasm as once he had. And she discovered he was no exception, that he was as selfish as other men, and more committed to his work, his vocation, than her. His patients absorbed and monopolised him as later his daughter did; and she should have been mature enough to cope. Not to give him Hassle.

Harriet ploughed her energies into the house. Her earlier ecstasy changed to a duller contentment. She tried not to compare the two. They went out in foursomes more often than as a couple, sometimes with Astrid and her husband. They discussed the Middle East, Ireland, drugs, the theatre . . . and Harriet surreptitiously observed her husband as he talked. She knew every gesture and nuance of expression and willed him to look in her direction, show some sign he was conscious of her beside him. When he did joy swept through her. But he was always supportive of her work and showed genuine interest in it, asked to see what she had done. She showed him every drawing, painting, preliminary sketch, collage. Sometimes she found him riffling through her sketch book. His comments were always considered and constructive and his interest encouraged her. What could she ask about his work in return? He told her that it didn't matter: he had no desire to discuss prostates or trapped nerves or psychosomatic backaches. But she would have liked to be more involved. She would have felt more equal.

In the summer they rowed on the river, Harriet wearing a skimpy red dress and wide-brimmed straw hat. Oliver caressed her bony back, uncluttered by straps from a brassière.

'Beautiful. You're so-o-o beautiful.'

Glorying in his compliment, she remembered how when she'd first met him she felt capable of tackling anything.

One evening he brought home a puppy; a lanky, long-eared, long-haired mongrel. 'It reminded me of you,' he teased her. 'Gangling and shaggy.'

'You say the most romantic things.'

They called the dog Pirate and when he ripped apart the cushions she was patient.

'You'll make a marvellous mother,' her husband said tenderly, running his cupped hand over the sweep of her pregnant belly.

Natasha was born. An early-autumn baby. Harriet was twenty-six.

'What were your feelings while you were pregnant?' the psychiatrist asks.

'Oh I was delighted. Very happy.'

'Why?'

• Valerie Blumenthal

'*Why*?' she repeats, puzzled as to what he means.
'Yes. For what reason were you delighted and happy?'
'Because . . . Well, because I wanted a baby.'
'Yes.'
She stares back at him, bewildered. 'Isn't that enough?'
'You haven't given me a reason, qualified your remark.'
'But it's natural to want a baby, isn't it?'
'For some women. Others have no maternal desire and make a conscious decision to remain childless. While *others* are ambivalent but have children for a number of reasons – guilt, because it's the right thing to do, because they believe it'll strengthen a shaky marriage . . .'
'Oh it was none of those things with me.' She smiles in relief, thinking this line of questioning to be finished with now.
But: 'Then, why were *you* happy to be pregnant?'
Harriet's face is the picture of confusion. Her eyes wander from him to the newly-sprayed plant on the table, the window, back to him, before settling on her own hands that had once longed to clasp a baby.
'I like babies. I like children. I wanted to have a child to hug and watch grow up and be friends with. Oliver's and my child. The seal on our relationship. Confirmation of our love to each other, if you like.'
Finally, she thinks he must be satisfied. But twin ridges have swelled the bridge of his nose.
'What would you say was the stronger in you, desire to bond your love with your husband, or desire to have a child to love for the child's sake?'
But she hadn't analysed it at the time. It had been the simplest, most natural decision made by both of them: Let's have a baby. Throw away the pill. They had a candle-lit, throw-away-the-pill celebratory dinner at home. Six months' supply into the dustbin along with the chicken carcass. Oliver had done her pregnancy test. He knew for

sure before she did, came back with the blue specimen in its little test tube and laid it on the breakfast-room table with a bunch of expensive, scentless red roses.

She can only say what she thinks she must have felt. 'Equal measures. I felt both desires equally.'

His eyebrows remain sunken a few seconds longer. 'Did you ever try to envisage the future?'

'Oh yes, often,' she answers, leaning forward enthusiastically.

'Can you describe it?'

And even as she describes it to him, she realises how hopelessly idealised it was, like a hackneyed television commerical.

'I know,' she says, giving a small wry laugh at the end of her account. 'Don't tell me. I know.'

'Was your own childhood like that?'

'No. Is anybody's? My mother was narrow-minded and bossy though well-meaning. Very Calvinistic. A stickler for detail. She was unaffectionate towards me, although not particularly strict. I would say she was – and still is – uninterested. She was the dominant one of my parents and my father and I just went along with what she said. Perhaps he was weak and that frustrated her. I've never considered that before. How odd. I've always wondered how he put up with her. I never saw my father as flawed.'

Suddenly she sees her own mother from a different aspect and feels faintly uncomfortable.

'I wanted a large family; several children,' she confides, picking at the plant's glossy leaves. 'When we were both – ready – I stopped taking the pill again. I miscarried. I didn't get pregnant after that. In a way—'

She breaks off and he probes, 'Yes?'

'Maybe it was as well. I don't know how Natasha would have reacted.'

'And yourself?'

'I don't know how I'd have coped if another child had turned out the same as Natasha. It would have been impossible. I think that concerned me. What am I saying? I know it did. I never told Oliver. He'd have been appalled. A lack in me. A sign of my own immaturity.'

Remembering: Natasha as a baby; and herself, blissful, loving her child sucking her darkened nipples, loving her own rounded body and full breasts. And the baby's eyes focusing on her, familiarising herself with her mother's features.

Oliver took photographs of them like that: mother and daughter, naked. He had them enlarged and framed and hung them on the breakfast-room walls for all to see. Several years later she took them down, embarrassed. Natasha was also embarrassed. She said they were disgusting, that they made her want to be sick.

'It's like being a cow,' she said. 'Why couldn't I just have had a bottle?'

The tantrums began when she was two and the parents differed on how she should be raised. He was progressive and indulgent. Harriet was stricter and instinctive. The screams pierced her ears, her head, and the hurling of objects to the floor, the constant defiance drove her to distraction. She had been unprepared for this. Oliver, the expert, claimed Natasha was frustrated by her inability to express herself; that she was advanced for her age and must be allowed to deal freely with her emotions. Harriet, too weary to theorise, her nerves frayed, smacked her once in front of Oliver. He rebuked her: she had demonstrated violence towards her own child and exercised her superior strength. She should be ashamed. She was being neurotic.

She was devastated by his criticism. She felt inadequate and a failure as a mother.

'Nat. Gnat,' he said, playing with the word. 'She looks like a gnat with her big eyes and small round face.' He called her Gnat from then on.

'What's the point of giving her a nice name then altering it?' Harriet asked.

'Look, you call her what you want. I'll call her what I want, all right?'

The child, aged two and three-quarters, played off mother against father.

'Daddy doesn't mind my toys on the floor,' she would say in her fluent speech and piping voice when Harriet told her to tidy them.

'What did I do wrong?' she asks the man studying her so intently. 'I hate mess. Dust, I don't mind. Mess, I hate. Why shouldn't she tidy her toys away, rather than automatically expecting me to? Oliver said I swamped her, was asserting my personality over hers, trying to make her into a replica. He said she must learn to do things freely. But what of basic right or wrong? I wasn't neurotic. I wasn't . . . And when I defended myself to him he just clammed up. It was a bad time. I hate thinking about it.'

Her composure has crumbled and she reaches for a Kleenex.

'I don't think there's anything wrong in expecting her to tidy her own things,' he says. And she smiles gratefully at him.

'I loved her, despite everything. She was so bright, could be so sweet and said the funniest things. And I tried so hard to make *her* love *me* that it almost became a goal. Occasionally, as a kind of hangover from childhood, I say my prayers, and I used to entreat God to make her love me . . . I feel terribly silly telling you that.'

He ignores the comment. 'You say you tried so hard. Do you think you tried too hard?'

'I don't know. Maybe.' But her only certainty is her sense of injustice.

'Children know when one is being artificial with them. Your tension might have been communicated to her and prevented you from being natural.'

'Yes it could be,' she agrees, reflecting on how she has always needed people to think well of her, even people she hardly knows.

'Your pride,' a boyfriend told her.

But it is not so. Her lack of self-confidence goes back to gauche childhood and demands reassurance that she is more loveable, more beautiful and talented than she gives herself credit. Her father had used to fill that niche.

Oliver's affair had begun. She did not know yet, but was baffled by the emergency call-outs and hospital meetings, committee meetings, seminars and conferences that removed him overnight. Weary Oliver, with his excuses and strained conversation and stained soul and ringed eyes that no longer gazed into hers.

Their love-making became less and less frequent and more perfunctory. Once he could spend what seemed like hours examining, caressing and licking her between her legs. Now only she did it to him, and then he would guide her head quickly upwards again.

'Don't you like it anymore?' she dared ask him eventually.

'Yes of course.'

'Then—'

'It's late. I'm tired. You don't seem to realise, I have a long day.'

So do I, she wanted to retort, but didn't. Tears for what had been slithered from under her closed lids, while safely on his patch of the bed he fell quickly asleep.

She devoted herself to her volatile daughter, attempted to elicit affection from her. But he was the one to whom she ran. Her whole being seemed to ignite with pleasure when she saw him, and he reserved his humour and demonstrativeness for this child who thought him the most perfect person on earth, as Harriet had done. But Gnat's image will remain forever untarnished, and to her detriment Harriet will not correct her. She knows what it means to be cherished by a father . . .

'When Natasha was three I finally discovered my husband's affair,' she says, gripping the corners of the seat, her features and hair blanched by the ribbon of sunlight. And this time the psychiatrist doesn't deflect her, but nods, indicating for her to continue.

It was the middle of the night and the telephone rang with an emergency call. Oliver searched in his appointment and address book for the number of a specialist, but the man was away on holiday, and he drove off, leaving the book by the phone.

She couldn't go back to sleep. Cold air had flooded into the bed where he had thrown back the duvet. She worried about him driving in the fog when he was tired. She went downstairs to make a cup of tea, filled a hot-water bottle and returned to bed. For something to do she looked in the book her husband had left behind.

The letter C. kept recurring. Everyone else was named, but C. was always C.

She kicked aside the hot-water bottle, sweating suddenly; enlightened. And she knew that her suspicions were not groundless as she cast her mind back over the past few months.

At the end of the book were names and telephone numbers: Mr; Mrs; a 'sir' – A 'Sir' who went NHS; Miss. And one without any prefix: C. Caroline. Caroline Anderson.

In this room which dredges the past from her and reverberates with secrets, Harriet twists about on the edge of her chair, then gets up and goes to the window, blocking the ribbon of light. So much has happened since that night. Oliver is no longer there, Elliot is; but the hurt is fresh and grating.

Past midnight, and she phoned Caroline Anderson. It was an irrational thing to do, but she was not feeling rational. The voice which answered was groggy with sleep. Harriet was weak with dread and momentarily her tongue stuck to the roof of her dry mouth. She couldn't speak.

'Who is it?' the voice enquired a second time.

'Harriet Edwards,' she replied. 'Oliver's wife.'

The weighty silence the other end told her all she needed to know, and she replaced the receiver; incredulous; in pain; freezing once more.

The fifth principal event of her adult life.

She grabbed the hot-water bottle from the floor and hugged it to her, as now she is hugging herself. She has only herself.

• • •

Gnat's been here seventeen whole days. She finds herself longing for ordinary things: to go to a supermarket and choose her favourite items: a tub of satay sauce, chocolate spread, Mars ice creams, her favourite cereal. She wants to be in her own room with the patchwork cover made by Harriet on the bed, and her collection of pigs amongst her books, and scarves and jewellery hanging from the mirror. Her cello. But the strings are severed; she cut them in a temper. She cries a lot nowadays. Not since her father died has she cried so much.

She is reconciled to this place already, partakes in the daily routine like an old hand: up at eight o' clock, dress, breakfast in the open-plan dining room: one big happy family, The Spoon says cheerfully; Nurse Spooner with the aptly long, dished face.

One big happy family: twenty adolescents between the ages of twelve and eighteen, all loused-up, pretending not to be, some more loopy than others. Kids who steal, kids with tattoos and pimples and railway braces on their teeth. Strapping sixteen-year-old Janine who never stops washing and writes poetry nobody understands; Craig who won't go near water; Lisa with one leg shorter than the other, who wears Doc Martens because she has to, who wouldn't say boo to anyone, but has set fire to three different foster homes; huge, crop-haired John who nailed his bedroom furniture to the floor and cannot sleep unless his shoes are exactly aligned and every cupboard, every drawer properly closed. They sit down to breakfast at two tables with four nurses they call by Christian names, and collect their food from the counter if it's cold and through the hatch if it's hot. A couple of girls refuse to eat. If they do, they rush off afterwards to be sick. Usually a nurse catches them in time. They might pretend to be friends, the nurses, but they are vigilant; everything one does is noted and reported.

After those early disbelieving, screaming days when she had to be sedated and slept on her own, Gnat calmed down and sussed it all out; sleeps now in a dormitory with four other girls: Maria, Cheryl who suffers from bulimia, Alice who has a phobia about blue and Susan who is always looking over her shoulder because she thinks someone or something is about to pounce on her. Apart from Maria and Cheryl, Gnat mostly keeps to herself, although occasionally she side glances at one of the boys there. Robert is fifteen, slight and handsome, and traumatised after being sexually assaulted by a lorry driver from whom he had hitched a lift. This according to Maria, who seems to know everything. He has been in Turner's End for six weeks and not uttered a word.

Maria looks more saintly than ever, the taupe smudges beneath her azure eyes blending into the oyster of her

• Valerie Blumenthal

skin. Two days ago, having no access to pills, she crammed poisonous berries from a shrub into her mouth and was found writhing on the tennis court.

After breakfast they make their beds, and from half past nine lessons are held in an annexe in the grounds. Gnat is easily the brightest, cleverer than the fifteen- and sixteen-year-olds. Learning for her is a pleasure and effortless, and the others regard her enviously. There is no homework, and at half-past three they return to the main building and can do what they want. She cannot believe the freedom: a safe kind of cossetting freedom. Nothing is expected of her.

Jason hovers around as she sorts through a pile of magazines and she gives him a V-sign. He grins without comprehension and momentarily, momentarily she feels a lurch of pity towards him. Eventually she selects *Hatter's Castle* from the bookshelves.

'What do you want with a boring book like that?' asks Cheryl, peering at it. Gnat is about to give an insulting reply, then can't be bothered.

In the games room adjoining the recreation room there is a ping-pong table as well as pool, and John, looking more as though he is fencing, is playing against Janine, whose face glows with a mixture of infatuation and exertion. One big happy family. And how easy to escape. Others do. It's common knowledge, though quite often they come back voluntarily. Maria says she and a couple of girls have even gone picking up boys sometimes. So who is to prevent Gnat? The doors aren't locked, neither are the gates bolted. Nothing to stop her re-entering the world of normality as opposed to the one which masquerades. But she is oddly reluctant. And where would she go? Sometimes she wanders beyond the boundaries of the adolescent home, a short distance up the road to the village, which is divided by a level crossing and has burgeoned around a few old crinkle-roofed buildings. There is an ugly precinct comprising a newsagent's and post office with hooks outside for tying dogs; a grocer's; a butcher's; an electrical shop; a bookie's, and a hairdresser's. Through the steamy plate window Gnat can glimpse women with rollers submerged beneath busby-hooded dryers, knitting or reading magazines; whilst through the open windows of the bookie's the commentator's excited voice gathers pace and sounds as though it is running away with him. Men wander in and out. They tend to be small and grubby and invariably check their money before entering. When the door opens cigarette smoke enshrouds the hazy figures within.

Sometimes a train tears past at the crossing and she is transported to a land of mountains and lakes and flower-strewn meadows, a place of such unearthly beauty that she stands with her eyes closed long after the sounds of the train hurtling away are distant.

Between the precinct and a Victorian pub is a narrow alleyway, and down here, backing onto playing fields, is a cabinet maker's workshop Gnat discovered while exploring. Peeping through the window, she saw a man planing a piece of wood, and he glanced up and waved. He had an old cheerful face beneath a shock of white hair. She was fascinated by carpentry, seeing people work with their hands, and, after deliberating a bit, she went inside. The workshop smelt of oil and wood and and was infused with light; curly shavings carpeted the floor and tools were scattered about. Furniture was stacked against a wall.

'Can I watch you?' she asked.

He looked at her and knew where she was from. Smiling, he nodded. 'If you'd like to.'

He began planing the wood again and, with his head bent, asked her name. She told him. His was Tom. His great-grandson was going to be three and he was making a rocking horse for his birthday. Gnat spotted the parts assembled in a corner: the rocker and legs. She thought of her old dappled-grey rocking horse; the thrill of seeing it in the hall on her birthday. Tears sprang to her eyes, and she rubbed them away.

'How old are you?' she asked the cabinet-maker.

'Seventy-four,' he replied equably.

'You could be a great-great-grandfather one day.'

'I could indeed, if the trend continues and the old man of the skies sees fit.'

She stood close to him, watching as he slotted pieces of wood together and glued minute pegs. His work was intricate. He was endlessly patient, but his fingers trembled and often it took a couple of attempts to place the pegs in holes. She was always relieved for him when they found their home. He asked her to pass him a screwdriver, and she was glad to be of use; a glow spread within her. He offered her a biscuit later – and she realised it was tea. She was late for tea.

'I must go,' she told him, taking the currant biscuit he pushed at her on a cracked, patterned plate.

'Come and visit me again,' Tom said.

'OK.'

She ran down the hill, sweetly, strangely invigorated.

Since then she has been there twice and a friendship has developed between them. She likes the fact he doesn't ask her questions about herself and accepts her as she is. Nor is he condescending like so many adults. Last time she was there he had brought his Jack Russell terrier with him especially to show her. Gnat picked it up and it licked her face with a fishy-smelling tongue. She giggled and pushed his nose away. 'Ugh, he's stinky,' she said.

'He's on some new diet,' Tom explained. 'He was getting fat, the wife said, so she gives him this new stuff which pongs to high heaven.'

'Won't he cut his paws on nails and things?' Gnat asked.

'Nah! You watch, he'll go straight and lie on that old

jacket of mine once you put him down. He'll not budge from it.'

Gnat carried him over to Tom's blue jacket on the floor by the workbench and set him on it. The little dog circled a few times then lay down and began growling. Gnat laughed. 'Why's he doing that?'

'He's guarding it, aren't you, Toby? Sharp as anything, that dog is.'

'We've got a spaniel at home. He's cute, but I miss my first dog. Pirate, his name was. He was run over.'

'Now that's a shame. Still, he'll be up among the clouds now, playing with all his mates.'

'Do you believe that?'

''Course. Don't you?'

'I don't know. Sort of. I want to.'

'Wanting to's as good as anything,' Tom said, with one of those profound finger wags of his.

In the dormitory now, for something to do, she changes round the position of her posters on the wall by her bed, sorts her bits in the chest of drawers, re-arranges her photos: her father; Pirate; Dimple; and herself riding. She settles down to read *Hatter's Castle*. This is her home. One big motley happy family. *This* is her home. It has happened that way. Because of things.

• • •

'She was an ex-girlfriend,' Harriet says. 'Everything I'm not. Placid, self-assured, efficient. She must have been like a balm. A no-hassle balm. I don't know how he had time.'

This is their third session and he notices the physical changes in her, her honey-brown cheeks and easing of the tension lines running to her mouth.

'How are you feeling?' he asks, stalling her from her random thoughts.

'I do nothing but sleep,' she answers. 'Sleep and more sleep.'

'You're looking better.'

'Am I? I suppose I must be. Better. My fiancé, Elliot, he's very supportive. I'm scared—' she breaks off and bites her lip.

'Yes?'

She gives a laugh, trying to make it sound flippant. 'I'm scared it will all prove too much for him and he'll leave me.'

Waiting for it to happen as a kind of inevitability; almost willing it, to get it over and done with. It was unrealistic to expect someone to remain under such circumstances. He couldn't be blamed. She prepares herself for that day, for the solitude ahead. Even when he tells her he adores her, that she is sweet and funny, beautiful and brave she knows he will leave. When they chose the ring and he put it on her finger she knew it would not be there permanently. When he makes love to her and his eyes drill into hers as he luxuriates in her body, and her warm flesh seals round his, her long legs and arms twining round him, trapping him for extended moments at least – even then she knows he will tire of the whole business, of her, of complications and of love.

'Why do you have such a low opinion of yourself?' the psychiatrist asks.

'Do I? Maybe I have a low opinion of men.'

Her own words make her sit up with surprise. She hasn't considered this before, has always thought of her own failings, that she is ungainly and unloveable. At school she was hopeless at sports.

'You're so clumsy, just like your father,' her mother used to say, clearing up some spillage for which Harriet was responsible. 'No leave it. You'll only make it worse. I'll do it.' And Harriet would look on, arms hanging uselessly at her side while her mother knelt down and made a great show of scrubbing . . .

'Every man is different,' he says, 'just as every woman and every child is. Don't you see that a man of strong character and maturity wouldn't be threatened by your problems, by this crisis in your life, but would wish to help you?'

'He must yearn for peace and quiet and instead find himself swept up by this crazy household.'

He crosses his short legs, and she smiles fleetingly, at his furry eyebrows and gnome-like bulbous nose, then is immediately serious.

'I can't believe his love will endure.'

'Don't you think that in the right partnership we all have it in us to love enduringly and be loved enduringly?'

'I don't know. It seems so much to expect. So complicated. So – human.'

Had her father been a philanderer? He had been a big, virile-looking man before his stroke; had that been part of the problem with her mother, the reason she had doused her faded Celtic beauty in frigid virtue and disapproval? Or had her frigidity driven him away? Which, if either, had come first?

'I wanted to be faithful to my husband.'

But Caroline Anderson changed the pattern of things.

Out of the foggy night emerged her husband, tired and unsuspecting of what had been fermenting in his absence; to be greeted by a mad woman in her dressing-gown hurling herself upon him, shrieking incoherently and pummelling his chest.

'What is this, what on earth's happened to you?' he said, trying to capture her hands.

But rage had given her strength. She was a creature possessed; envisaging her husband lying in bed with, caressing Caroline Anderson, making love to her, kissing her between her legs; and the pair of them discussing her, Harriet, pitying her, criticising her for those inadequacies which had made Oliver turn away; making plans that did not include her.

'Have you gone crazy?' he asked.

'*You* have gone crazy,' she shrilled back. 'You and C – C.C.C. See? C. Caroline Anderson.'

She broke into sobs and he was stonily, frighteningly silent. For a few seconds she was also, then she began shrieking at him again.

'Well? Have you nothing to say?' Shriek, scream, flailing arms. She could hear herself, watch herself. She was quite ghastly – sufficient to drive him legitimately to her rival.

'No,' he replied in a tight tone, and this time caught her wrists, squeezing them. 'I've nothing to say. Not while you're like this.'

He released her abruptly, leaving her arms limp and longing to embrace and be embraced; leaving her longing to be told it was all a mistake and, wake-up, wake-up, it was a dream. But he brushed loftily past, as though she were in the wrong, as though it was her affair. He went upstairs, still wearing his coat; the fog, the frost damp on its fibres; into their daughter's room. She chased after him and yelled outside, enraged by his imperviousness towards her, his icy control.

'I'll tell your patients what you're like. I'll tell everyone.'

Downstairs she opened a bottle of champagne and drank the lot, finishing by pouring herself a Cointreau. After such an orgy of alcohol she was violently and agonisingly ill. In the bathroom her husband held her as she vomited unremittingly into the toilet. For hours he knelt beside her and stroked her drenched hair and forehead in a simulation of love and caring while she was hardly aware of him. Eventually he carried her, like a rag doll, to bed, to their bed, and himself slept in the spare room.

The next day he drove Natasha to nursery school. When

Harriet fetched her at lunchtime her daughter studied her shrewdly.

'I heard you being cross with Daddy last night,' she said.

'You must have dreamed it, darling.'

'I wasn't dreaming. I wasn't. He came into my room. He cuddled me.'

'Would you like to go to the park?'

Frail and nauseous, she watched as the little girl soared higher and higher on the swing, into the wintery air; then whirled round on the roundabout with other children. Her blurred face flashed by. Her hair was a banner. More, more. Oliver had wanted more than she could give him. And she had given her all.

Her pain settled into a knot within her and a few nights later husband and wife spoke together, calmly.

'He was in love with her when he had just taken his finals and she was in her last year at Oxford reading English,' Harriet says, sipping from the glass of water she requested earlier. 'He wasn't ready for it to finish, apparently.'

It strikes her how seldom relationships are synchronised.

'He met me when she had just gone abroad, teaching English in Indonesia. How do I compete with that? Teaching in Indonesia.'

'You don't have to compete. You have your own accomplishments.'

'She was more elusive than me, perhaps that was it.'

She has learned over the years that men find an enigmatic woman tantalising because she challenges their hunter's instincts. There is nothing enigmatic about Harriet.

'Oliver was obsessed by her and loved me, that was his explanation. He hadn't got over the obsession from years previously. She hadn't had time to slither from her pinnacle. She was very beautiful, I gather.'

Harriet stares through the window at the rain driving

down, and tosses her head back, revealing her long throat and laying claim to her own unorthodox beauty; her carved face of extraordinary planes and angles and shadows.

She had made the mistake of asking her husband, 'Is she beautiful?' And because he believed truth mattered now, although in this instance she would have preferred a lie, he had answered, 'Yes. Very.'

Did he have to embellish, to say, 'very'?

'What colour is her hair?'

'Black.'

And Harriet imagined her hair, inky, Asian-black hair, spread over the pillow.

'She went to Australia directly from Indonesia, and when she returned Oliver and I were married. When I discovered their affair I tortured myself thinking that our early married life had been a sham, that all the while he was with me he'd been wanting her.'

She puts her head in her hands — they clasp it like the cup round the nut of an acorn — and continues in a muffled tone, 'He should have told me at the time. He knew everything there was to about me, but I didn't know this important part of him. Later he admitted he was afraid it would have put me off . . .

'Anyway, they kept in touch by letter. She went to America, married an American and lived in New York where she was an editor for a large publishing house. When they divorced she returned to England and set up as a literary agent, got in touch with my husband. Knowing he was my husband. How can women do it to each other? Don't we owe each other more loyalty than to swipe each other's partners?'

Remembering: nights of sleeplessness, trying to comprehend, not knowing what to do for the best; condemning him, consoling him, threatening him, entreating him. And the pillow cold beside her because he was in the spare room; and her own, sodden from crying.

She was lethargic, had no energy to cook or clean the house or fight with her daughter; dragged herself to her classes and let her pupils behave like anarchists. And perversely longed for her husband; whom she called a shit and a bastard, to come home each evening, dreading that one day he wouldn't. Those weary doctor eyes of his begged for No Hassle, their dark circles evidence of his own suffering, albeit self-induced. Perhaps he had been with C. that day – Harriet would always think of her as C. Perhaps she had given him an ultimatum; no, she was too clever for that. Perhaps the more he saw of C. the sooner she would fall from grace and her ashes be laid to rest.

Meanwhile they discussed divorce.

'The sod. The lousy, fucking sod,' Astrid said when Harriet told her. She swore like a brickie in her refined voice which sounded as though she were reciting Shakespeare. She stroked her friend's thin cheeks.

'What's wrong with me?' Harriet asked plaintively.

'Nothing,' Astrid assured her fiercely. 'Nothing at all, darling. You're wonderful. If I were lesbian I'd fancy you. I wish I were lesbian. Fucking men. Fucking selfish sods. About ninety per cent of violent crimes are committed by men, you know that? Bloody "Y" chromosome. Scientists should find a way of removing it.'

She was having problems with her own marriage. Her husband who was in advertising, belittled her in public and was drinking heavily

Harriet told her father that Oliver had a mistress. She told him how purposeless, unwanted and unneeded she felt. She rested her head in his motionless lap while her mother and the nurse were out of the room. She wept onto his thighs. His distorted, rigid face didn't move, but his hands beneath hers were fluttering, and when she looked up great globules of tears stood out in his eyes.

But at least, as the weeks passed, they were talking. They were civilised. And now Harriet thought she knew everything there was to know but was so dulled by it she had ceased to care. She painted wild abstracts on huge canvasses and entered them in a local but prestigious competion. To her astonishment she won. Her photo, blurred and unflattering – she looked like Quasimodo, she joked to Astrid – was in the paper. Oliver seemed proud of her. She got on with her life. She told her husband, 'I can forgive you, but I can't excuse you.' She was wonderfully dignified.

They had done nothing about the divorce, were still husband and wife in title. Harriet taught her unruly pupils, painted her pictures and attended to her child politely. Never for a moment did she allow herself to think or feel; and a strange, distant peace hung over the unkempt house. Six months since that frosty foggy night when she had phoned up C.; and she would catch Oliver looking at her strangely. Without realising it, Harriet was being intriguing and elusive. And one night found Oliver in bed with her.

She lay scarcely daring to move, half feeling that he was intrusive as his fingers glided over her body, stroked her skin, her curves and swells and folds; and his mouth and tongue followed his fingers and then found her mouth. How long since he had done exactly this with C.? Her body was compliant: it let him in but was reserved in its response. Her brain protested, What gives you the right? Outwardly she was tranquil, the one in control.

'I love you,' he said, his penis prodding tenderly inside her. 'I really, really love you. I'm sorry. Oh God, I'm so sorry. I don't know what came over me.'

He was as gentle and as reverent as he had been so long ago, in the early days, and she was amazed to realise he was crying. He was back. Truly he was back. His affair, his obsession, was finished. C. was banished. But where was Harriet's victory?'

'Wrap your legs around me,' he murmured, his tears on her neck; and she obeyed, fastening her feet together on top of his buttocks. But where was her victory?

'I don't understand. I should have been glad,' she says.

'There can be no victory,' the psychiatrist comments, 'where there is disillusion.'

His words fill her with a sudden and extraordinary clarity. Her whole face lightens with it. 'Of course,' she exclaims, grabbing at the air with her hands. 'Why didn't I see that?' She had never acknowledged disillusion. Only anger. 'Of course, of course,' she repeats to herself, shaking her head.

He lets her settle down again, then asks, 'In what way would you say your marital problems affected your daughter?'

'I'm not sure. I tried not to let them affect her.'

'Don't you think she would have sensed a difference between you and your husband, and in your own mood?'

She hesitates and blushes. 'Truthfully, I was too wrapped up in myself to notice.'

He purses his lips without comment. Their time is up. 'This afternoon will be difficult for you,' he says.

She had forgotten. Enmeshed as she has been in the past, she had forgotten about this afternoon, which has preoccupied her thoughts for days.

'Elliot's taking me. I don't think I'd be capable of driving myself. He'll drop me off then fetch me. It was his idea.'

'He sounds like a considerate man.'

'He is.'

• • •

Three weeks. Three weeks today; and something shameful

has happened to Gnat, too shameful for her to confide to anyone; so far somehow, she has managed to conceal it. Since Dr Middleton told her about today's meeting with her mother she has wet her bed three consecutive nights.

She wakes as soon as she has done it, a saturated patch beneath her bottom. The first time she assumed it to be a unique accident and was not unduly bothered, the second she was mortified. She makes the bed quickly, before a nurse should see, careful to arrange the pillows neatly and keep the duvet smooth. At night she lies avoiding the clammy patches. She is disgusted at herself, can think of nothing but those wet circles.

'Are you all right Gnat?' The Spoon asks; her teacher asks, Maria asks, because she is so quiet.

'I'm fine. Leave me alone.'

She dreads this afternoon.

There was another time when she wet her bed. Her father had died and her mother announced they were moving to London.

'I'm not going. I'm not going,' she had shouted.

Everything she valued and that was familiar to her was collapsing, being removed. She was being removed. In the new house, a girl with developing breasts and the pale beginnings of pubic hair, she wet her bed. Her mother had been understanding, and in return, humiliated, she had hurled abuse at her. Harriet's wounded expression that Gnat believed was contrived to fill her with guilt, only incited her further. Her mother whisked off the sheet without another word and repeated the procedure . . .

It is pouring with rain, and the suburban Surrey hill with its dark curly trees is veiled with grey. The white gravestones merge into obscurity. The sea has vanished, and *she* is tempted to vanish, take refuge. She could go to Tom and listen to his stories of his boyhood, of an impossibly long time ago when his father played the piano in the pit at a cinema.

He has endless tales about it, so vivid that she can visualise the distorted pictures on the screen, hear the groans of the audience at the appearance of a rash of brown spots or zig-zag streaks, the crackles, the whirring, and the tinny piano. He draws on his pipe as he chats and works and she is content simply to watch and listen, his voice floating over her. She has started revealing things to him also; snippets. 'Is that so?' he'll say, sometimes with perplexity in his tone. Or, 'My, my.' And, 'It were all different in my day,' he said once. 'You know I never saw my mam set foot out the house without putting her gloves and felt hat on. Secured with a little pearl hatpin. Them were gracious days. Even if you was poor. Safe days. Folks was courteous to one another then. Had time for a chat or to give a bit of advice. It's all rush nowadays. Rushing and mugging. I don't know.'

Gnat remains where she is, her stomach churning, looking at the rivulets of rain chasing each other down the window; waiting, convincing herself, 'I hate her, I hate her, I hate her.' A stale litany to which she rocks out of rhythm.

Her knickers are wet, and the wetness is down her thighs. Distressed, she dashes to the lavatory upstairs and there locks herself in.

3

Gnat carries the stool over to the high window in the bathroom and clambers onto it, enabling her to see out and keep vigil. Her heart will not quieten.

Five minutes pass and she is stiff and bored, perched there with nothing to distract her. Then she hears a car slowing behind the long hedge bordering the road, and it crunches into the drive. She recognises the throaty sound of the engine even before she sees that Elliot is driving: his old XK150 that, after Harriet, is the love of his life. Gnat can decipher her outline beside him, and their forms join briefly as they kiss, like a Victorian silhouette cut-out. Then her mother is emerging from the car, tall and reed-slim in faded jeans and ballet pumps and a long cardigan, her loose hair wispy, jagged-edged. She doesn't look like an ordinary mother.

Biting her nails, Gnat watches her walk towards the main building then stop to wave to Elliot, who blows her a kiss through the open window and drives off. Harriet's shoulders are instantly forlorn, and she gazes around, her eyes sweeping over the bathroom window. Gnat ducks, and slips from the stool, and by the time she has climbed back her mother has disappeared from sight.

She imagines Dr Middleton discussing her progress with Harriet and becomes more wrought-up thinking about it.

And what do they know? They aren't her, can't get in her head, however they try. But at least she is cured of Elliot: when she saw his car nosing into the drive she felt nothing.

She should be downstairs. They will be waiting for her. But she can't go. For three days and nights she has thought about this afternoon's meeting, has wet her bed because of it, and now she can't possibly go into that room and face her mother.

Someone is outside the bathroom.

'Gnat.' The Spoon, cheery as if nothing's amiss. 'Your mother's here.' As if she doesn't know.

And how did The Spoon guess where she was? Nothing escapes their notice in this place. She is their business, their property.

She doesn't answer, goes over to the toilet and tries to wee, but there's nothing left. She wishes she had a book to read; or a pen so she could scrawl on the wall. Everyone does. It's always washed off. She has an hour to pass stuck in this boring bathroom, with only her thoughts to occupy her and her pounding heart. Perhaps it will burst – erupt and splatter through her skin. And a picture flashes before her of the events of that evening when her mother told her she was going to marry Elliot.

From outside the door comes the creaking of floorboards as The Spoon shifts from one foot to the other. 'Gnat dear, they're waiting for you downstairs.'

No reply.

A fly buzzes frantically in a spider's web strung between two pipes, and Gnat is about to release it when she realises she would be depriving the spider of his food; he might die of starvation. The buzzing sounds like a light bulb before it expires, and tears well in her eyes as she witnesses the fly's struggle. Outside, the floorboards reveal The Spoon's restlessness.

'Gnat, please unlock the door.'

Gnat. Nat. Natasha. Natasha, how could you have put that thing in your nostril? Natasha, where did you get hold of those cigarettes? Natasha, why, why, why? Leave me alone. Leave me alone. Her mother waiting for her to appear. Her mother bleeding because of Gnat. Her dress – that sweet, ancient, skimpy dress, redolent of picnics by the river – is red.

Gnat is shivering. The fly is buzzing. The Spoon goes away, her footsteps light down the corridor until they can no longer be heard.

Minutes later there are masculine, purposeful ones along the corridor, stopping outside the bathroom.

'Gnat.' Dr Middleton's voice filters through; golden-coaxing. 'You don't have to say anything, but just so that I know you're OK, will you knock on the door?'

Slowly, like an automaton, she goes over to it and raps three times.

'Well that's something at least.'

She can almost hear him smiling. It occurs to her they might have thought she'd done herself in. Would they have cared?

'Won't you come out? It's important you come down and talk. Of course you're anxious. It's natural you should be. But your mother wants to see you. She's anxious too, you know.'

She doesn't answer, is sitting on the stool, taking gulping breaths and fighting the urge to scream with disappointment. The screams rise to her throat and remain anchored, and overcome with giddiness she puts her head between her knees. Her ears are buzzing like the distraught fly.

'If you change your mind we'll be in the usual room. Please consider it.'

She can't. She can only think about that terrible, terrible evening with her mother. And her father's image reproaches her.

'Why are you in bed? What's wrong with you?' she had asked him during his illness, frightened by him lying there, daily more yellow.

'Because I'm a big silly,' he answered.

Once his eyes were closed when she went into the room, sealed tight like shells, and she thought he was dead. She shook him. 'Daddy. Daddy.'

They opened and he smiled at her, and she started laughing in relief. 'You're okay, you're okay.' She cuddled up to him.

'Of course I am, soppy thing.'

'Mummy's crying. She says it's onions she's peeling, but I know she's crying.'

And he said to her, 'Be nice to Mummy.'

'I am nice.'

'Really nice, I mean. She loves you very much.'

Dr Middleton goes away. His footsteps sound dispirited but it is simply beyond Gnat's will or power to go downstairs. And she left a wet patch in the chair. The Spoon will have seen it. And the kids. They saw her sitting there and will know it was her, will know she wets herself like a baby. John will rag her. He always rags her.

Time ticks slowly by. She undoes her watch and hurls it at the wall: its hands are moving too slowly. Young boistrous voices carrying. A boy laughing. He sounds really happy. How can he be happy? And in the bathroom, the buzzing of the wretched trapped fly. Unable to stand it any longer, she breaks the web and the insect is freed. Reprieved, it darts round the room and settles on the window, which she opens; it flies off into the rainy sky. The spider will spin another web, and another insect will be captured in it, but she, Gnat, will not have to be party to its suffering. A gnat in a web.

* * *

Remembering: the last time Dimple came to stay in London, when they quarrelled the entire weekend. Dimple was still living in Windsor and had her own pony. Gnat had been expelled from her school in Kensington, and the world of gymkhanas was far removed. She was bitterly envious of her friend, had the urge to strike out spitefully at her.

'Windsor's boring,' she said. 'London's much better. London's cool.'

'You're fibbing. You're just saying it. I know when you're just saying things.'

'I'm not just saying it. Windsor's – bourgeois.' She'd heard her mother use the word.

'I've got a new friend called Camilla. Her mother's a lady, or a countess or something.'

'Bully for her and bully for you. Quel draggy drag. I hate your new hairstyle. It makes your face look fat.'

'It doesn't. Everybody likes it.'

'They're just saying it to be nice. Fatty-face, fatty-face. You look fat.'

'Well you look like a pig with that thing in your nose.'

'You just don't know what's cool. You're too bourgeois to know.'

When Dimple left Gnat was in despair, sorrowed at the loss of her best friend, sorrowed over Windsor, over gymkhanas.

In one of their sessions Dr Middleton asked, 'What do you feel about your quarrel with her now? Do you regret it?'

And she answered in the tiniest voice, 'Yes.'

'Uhuh,' he nodded, appraising her. 'So?'

'So? I don't know what you mean,' she said, shaking her head.

'You started the quarrel. You directed it,' he told her. 'To a great degree we can direct our own lives and there's nothing to prevent your redirecting it in this instance. Nothing to stop your writing, explaining how you felt, as you have done to me.'

'I couldn't.'

Nonetheless her soul was momentarily lightened. He caught the change in her eyes, and laced his hands.

'I want to go back to Windsor. I hate living where we do.'

'You think that would make everything all right? Magic everything well again?'

She clenched her jaw and fought against crying, and he leaned forward and tapped her forehead with his index finger.

'In here, Gnat,' he said, 'not in Windsor, will we find the answer. And we shall find it. We're getting there.'

He gave her his own clean handkerchief for her tears which rolled slowly down her pale, pale face . . .

The hour is almost up. Soon Elliot will arrive to fetch her mother. And suddenly Gnat recalls one of their conversations. He was driving to school and she was leaning towards him, so proud to be beside him, to be in his car which made the other kids jealous; so happy because she had him to herself.

'Elliot, do you think I'm pretty?'

'Chump. Of course I do. But it shouldn't matter. Looks shouldn't matter.'

'But they do, don't they? Everyone knows that. You get what you want if you're pretty.'

'Beauty's in the eye of the beholder and all that.'

'Huh!' She moved away from him and sat back.

'Well, for what it's worth *I* think you're pretty. You'd be particularly good news without that ridiculous stud.'

'At school lots of girls have them. Some of the boys too.' She hesitated then blurted out, 'Elliot, I love you.'

'Well I love you.'

'I mean proper love.' She pulled out the cigarette lighter from its socket in the dashboard and slotted it back in.

'I mean proper love too. Like a daughter.'
'But I'm not your daughter.'
'No, but that's how I love you.'
'I want to marry you.'
'Chump. Who's a chump?' He took his left hand from the steering wheel to ruffle her blue, orange and red hair. 'And as for your hair,' he said . . .

Through the window she can see his car easing into the drive. He switches off the engine and sits there reading the paper propped against the windscreen. How boring. Why do men have this thing about reading the papers? Even her father did. Sundays present a real challenge – pages and sections spread out everywhere on the floor, and an irritable response if you dare interrupt.

Her mother appears, bowed and dejected-looking. Dr Middleton is with her, his hand on her arm as though consoling her. Has he sided with her? Has he ganged up on her, Gnat? Harriet climbs into the car, and Gnat sees her shaking her head when Elliot turns to her. The engine is started, emits that deep-throated gurgle, and the old Jaguar moves off. Back to London.

Gone. Her mother is gone. For three days Gnat has primed herself for this occasion and it has not transpired. She unlocks the door and slips out of the bathroom and into her dormitory, where she lies aching, aching, aching on the bed.

Someone comes in: The Spoon, concerned, caring; no recriminations.

'Your mother asked me to give you this,' she says in her even voice with the faint North Country accent, and leaves.

Gnat looks at the small pouch that has been placed beside her on the bed, and opens it. Inside is a silver charm bracelet. No note. One of the charms is a tiny dog with a ball in its mouth.

She holds the bracelet and gazes into space. She feels

utterly isolated, longs for the safety of her old anger and tries to muster it up; but the fabric of her anger has changed and become frail as eggshell containing the brick-weight of emotions breaking through.

I hate her, she reminds herself tiredly, clutching the bracelet, hanging on to it for her life's worth.

'Was she cross I didn't see her?'
'Don't you think she would have a right to be?'
'I suppose so.'
'Would you mind if she were cross?'
'I don't know.'
'Yes you do.'
'Look stop getting at me. Just stop getting at me, will you?' she shouts.

Her stud has fallen out. She has searched everywhere but can't find it. Her brown hair, newly washed, is dandelion fluffy.

Studying her intently, Dr Middleton says, 'In fact she wasn't cross. Only sad.'

The light gone from her mother's face; her mouth no longer uptilted. And she can suddenly hear Harriet laughing with Astrid over some shared joke; the pair of them like two young girls. Her mother's laughter is generous and warm.

'She hates me.'
'No, Gnat. You hate her.'

Gnat picks her nails. She thinks back to once when she was ill and Harriet brought her hot drinks in bed and read to her from *The Little Prince*; both of them howling over the ending together.

'Don't you?' he presses.

'I don't know. How do I know?' she mutters. 'You muddle me. Everyone's muddling me.'

'The trouble was, Gnat,' he says conversationally, 'you were jealous of your father showing love to your mother.

The jealousy persisted after he'd died. These things become a habit. But love isn't ownership, you know. It doesn't mean exclusivity. In a family it means sharing.'

She glares at him. 'She's made you side against me.'

'Not at all. She hasn't said anything bad against you, although you have against her.'

'Oh she's so great. I'm so horrible and she's so great. That's what everyone thinks.'

'Well make them unthink it about yourself. What about your father; what would you say were his faults?'

'He didn't have any.'

'You don't think he ever did anything wrong?'

'No.'

'Gnat, you're an intelligent girl, don't you think perhaps you're being a little unrealistic?'

'Daddy was perfect,' she insists.

'And your mother?'

'She, she—' Gnat moves about restlessly on the chair; she sees Harriet's illuminated gaze and abstracted gesticulating hands. 'She nagged. Always on at me about something. Always double-checking on me. Always getting me to tidy things.'

'Perhaps she was trying to guide you. And it was her home. Perhaps it wasn't agreeable for her to live in a mess. She has a career – don't you think it's fair to share the chores? You say she didn't respect you. Did you respect her?'

'Why are you getting at me today? She's turned you against me. She *has*.' Gnat bursts into tears. 'Everyone gets at me. Everyone hates me. I'm ugly. I hate my tits. I wish I didn't have them. I wish I was skinny like her. I wish I could kill myself.'

'Do you wish you'd killed your mother that evening?'

'No – yes – no. I hate you. I hate you all.' She flees the room. Out, out into the grounds. Craig and John are trying

• Valerie Blumenthal

to chat up Janine and Cheryl by the pavilion and nobody takes any notice of her. A sparrow shakes out wet feathers over the bird-bath. From somewhere comes the whine of an electric saw, which makes her think of Tom. The puddles on the tennis court are steaming in the warm sun. And she stares hard at the hill and the gravestones, and breathes deeply of the sea.

• • •

'It was his turn to be the giver,' Harriet says.

Four days have passed since the afternoon of her abortive meeting with her daughter. They have covered that – her disappointment and hurt – and are now discussing the period following Oliver's affair.

'Any contribution to the marriage had to be his,' she says.

Oliver bought her flowers, took her to the theatre and wooed her. In return she was kind and friendly. That was how she felt towards him. Besides a muted contempt. Nightly he poured his love into her with the zest of a newly-wed bridegroom. Once she had stifled her moans in the pillow or against his shoulder, now there was nothing to stifle. Her body felt private. She felt private. Sex was pleasant and left her unmoved, and if she could be bothered she had an orgasm; in silence. Sometimes in the day she would masturbate so that she would not have to give him the pleasure of her pleasure later on.

He took her to Paris for her birthday. When they left their daughter at Dimple's she refused to kiss either of them goodbye. But her scowl was reserved for Harriet. It was her mother's fault her father was leaving her behind.

They stayed in a converted abbey and had dinner at a brasserie-bar overlooking the canal, where a string quartet played as they ate.

'I must have been mad,' Oliver said, gazing at his wife, drunk with the ambience and with Corelli. 'You're everything a man could want. Yes,' he added in his most logical voice, 'It was a kind of madness.'

The next day they visited the Musée d'Orsay and afterwards had Caesar salads and pommes frîtes at a pavement café. They agreed it was strange London's attempts at café society had failed on the whole, and planned where the ideal place would be. They talked about literature – she was better read than him, and art, where they were equals, and music, which was his strength; lively, intelligent conversation.

'You're so stimulating,' he said.

'And what about C?' she thought cynically. She was conscious all the time of a wariness towards him. He had killed something within her which she could not, did not wish to, resurrect.

Three years passed. Oliver's attentiveness had worn thin again.

'It's odd,' she muses. 'We were two essentially nice people with plenty in common and yet we couldn't sort things out. I suppose we should have seen a counsellor. The marriage was stagnant. You must know what I mean? That apathy in a relationship. Maybe it was me; yes I know a lot of it was me. I had a husband for whom I couldn't rid myself of the old anger and – as you've explained to me – disillusion. And of course there was my daughter, to whom I couldn't get close, no matter what I did. Honestly, the dog gave me the most uncomplicated joy. He was a sweet dog, a real character. It was ghastly when he was run over. Natasha went crazy.'

She gives a short laugh. 'God, for the first time since I've been coming here I can see myself from a detached point of view, sitting here pouring out my life story like a sugar sifter. Pouring out my innermost self, spouting the first rubbish that comes to mind.'

'None of it's rubbish. It's all valid.'

'It is to me,' she says earnestly. 'Such a little, unremarkable life really, but valid to me.'

The psychiatrist leans forward slightly. 'The obvious key to your relationship with your daughter is the relationship you both had with her father,' he tells her. 'I'm sure you recognise that fact. From there stems everything: competitiveness, resentment, rivalry. Once a pattern had been established it was hard to break.'

Harriet had long ago come to this conclusion herself, then put it to rest, along with those other things she feared to confront. Now a sudden realisation makes her gasp out loud, and patchy colour spreads hotly over her face. How, she wonders, could she have failed to see the analogy before? It is so glaringly apparent: the analogy between her situation with her parents, and the one with her daughter. Is it relevant, she asks him?

'It may help you to understand your daughter better,' he answers carefully.

'And my mother. But she excluded me, not the other way round. With myself and Natasha I'm the one . . . Oh God, I can't work it out.'

Then back floods all the guilt, her self-doubts. 'Am I a bad mother? Should I have coped better?'

'I wouldn't say you were a bad mother at all. There is no yardstick. And as for coping better: everyone reacts differently to different situations. But it's especially hard to deal with conflict within the family, to be objective. One tends to act instinctively, whereas theoretically one should stand back a little, make a plan, even. I suspect that in your instance you were afraid to sit down with your little girl. You could have said, "Look, Natasha, let's talk about our differences and have them out. I want you to know that I love you, just as I do Daddy. And Daddy loves both of us too." Perhaps then you could have gone on to talk about the importance of sharing love. I'm not guaranteeing it would have worked, but it might have just broken the ice. Do you think you feared that by speaking out you would risk disturbing things and making them worse?'

Harriet clicks her thumb and forefinger together with an excited snap. 'Yes I was – you're right, I was.'

Then comes the inevitable weeping and she reaches for a Kleenex. Now she takes this as par for the course and after giving her nose a trumpeting blow, continues:

'It was a constant battle of wills between us. I resented her and I was afraid of her. She was so strong, so dominant. But I couldn't admit any of it. It seemed absurd. Abnormal. You can't believe how I envied normal families. Just seeing a little girl holding her mother's hand or hugging her made my eyes water. So I camouflaged my true emotions and pretended to myself as much as to her. But I used to seethe inwardly sometimes. She used to flaunt her bond with her father. I felt utterly superfluous. And for a while after his affair things were worse, as part of me couldn't be bothered to make any effort. Let them get on with it, I thought. I wouldn't admit to anyone things weren't right. Even Astrid didn't know how bad the difficulties were between Natasha and myself. It's such a mammoth admission, isn't it? To fail as a mother. The most natural role of all supposedly, and I fail at it.'

'You have not failed. You did not fail. You must rid yourself of that negative idea,' he reprimands her.

She can remember Oliver saying to her, 'You're still bitter towards me, aren't you?'

But he had his ringed eyes and his weary, don't-give-me-Hassle voice, and it was simpler to deny it. And in a way she wanted the bitterness to be there. An armour. She went on bluffing.

With his daughter he expressed that old ease, that open-hearted laughter, that interest he used to with Harriet.

Oliver had neither the time nor inclination to diagnose the ailments of his marriage. Just as she was afraid to open the Pandora's box of Natasha's mind and expose the gremlins there, so Oliver was with his wife. They drifted on as thousands of couples did, not malcontented, and occasionally even feeling a certain tenderness for one another. But their early rapport, their closeness and shared idealism had become the needle's eye of the past.

'I don't know where I'd have been without my friends,' she says.

She reflects on friendship and in particular sharp, soul-boosting Astrid.

While Harriet's marriage stagnated Astrid was in the throes of divorce. Her husband, who was considerably older and should have remained a bachelor, claimed she'd tricked him into marriage in the first place. When he had broken off their engagement her response had been to send two hundred and fifty wedding invitations to everyone she could think of, requesting that replies and gifts be sent to her fiancé's address. The ensuing complications made it simpler to marry. But triumph was short-lived.

'You can't capture them,' Harriet said. 'They won't be captured.'

Over a litre of wine they slayed men.

'Edward's entire life was spent in preparation for being a fifty-year-old,' Astrid remarked of her husband, and both women erupted into laughter. 'I know this woman,' she went on, 'she's a really tough-nut Chinese with long red nails – well her husband was having an affair and you know what she did? She found out when his assignments were and beforehand doused his coffee with sleeping pills. After several missed meetings the mistress gave up.'

'Oh God that's brilliant,' squealed Harriet, and they burst into laughter again.

Too drunk to drive home, she phoned Oliver and spent the night with Astrid, in the four-poster bed; both of them naked, Astrid's large breasts comfortingly squashed against her small ones. The two women touched each other curiously, briefly, and decided it wasn't for them.

'Fuck my heterosexuality,' Astrid muttered. 'Fuck men.' Before falling asleep, her body pressed innocently, sisterly against Harriet's.

A few weeks later Harriet began her affair.

'I was thirty-three and I felt not a moment's guilt. Not a qualm,' she tells the psychiatrist, looking defiantly at him. But his small nod makes her smile.

He was a writer in his early twenties. A tall, beautiful boy with hair almost as long as hers; glossy-clean, brown hair tied back in a pony tail. His face was that of Edward Burne-Jones' warrior in the painting, *Le Chant d'Amour*: olive-toned with a poet's heavy-lidded dreamer's eyes.

They met, improbably, at an otherwise conventional party given by a councillor and his wife, a couple in their mid-fifties, whose daughter had invited some friends of her own. Amongst this group, smoking moodily, slightly apart from the others and wearing a faintly mocking, supercilious expression, was Christos. He stared at Harriet as she entered the room and she caught his eye, looked away, then stared back, intrigued. With their gaze still held, he wove his way gracefully through the roomful of people to reach her. Oliver was speaking to their host.

'Who are you?' the boy asked Harriet urgently, 'I have to see you again.'

She laughed softly. 'Don't be silly.' And looked round to make sure no one was listening.

'No, I mean it. Where's your sense of romance?'

She feigned a moue of sadness. 'My sense of romance deserted me at about the stage your voice was breaking.'

'That's a patronising remark,' he said. 'And the timing of

our births was accidental and is irrelevant. You are actually ageless and so am I. Some people are like that. Not many. Writer,' he added, pointing to himself.

'Artist,' she said, pointing to herself with the same seriousness and trying not to laugh.

He was not yet twenty-four. His mother was Greek and had once sung in bars, and was divorced from his father, an archaeologist whom Christos had accompanied on many of his expeditions. He was interested in Egyptology and mythology and his books were allegorical, he told her. She learned all this in their first ten minutes in the corner into which he steered her. He blamed the fact his books weren't published on publishers' 'myopia'. 'My books are exploratory,' he declared airily, with a wave of his pale, long-fingered hand. 'Publishers are so staid.'

And in the interim, she asked, smiling, how did he earn a living?

He accused her again of being patronising and told her – flushing and shamefaced – that he worked part-time at a local winebar. And this faltering admission, his boyish blushing, made up for his pseudo-intellectual posturing. She felt protective towards him.

'One day you'll do what you really want to,' she said.

'I can't believe it'll ever happen,' he said, stripped bare of all pretence now. 'Sometimes I think I'll be in that bloody wine bar for ever.' He looked agonised. 'When can I meet you again? Where?' he asked.

'Soon.' She glanced towards Oliver who had been watching her disapprovingly but was now deep in conversation with a local solicitor, and hurriedly she scrawled her phone number on a page of her diary which she ripped out.

'What have I done, what have I done?' sang her head all the way home in the car, while beside her, in the driver's seat, Oliver was taciturn. In fact she knew exactly what she had done and what she intended to do. Even at this stage she felt a sense of satisfaction as she looked at her husband's stern profile: revenge.

'It was primitive, that need for revenge,' Harriet says. 'I didn't think I was like that. Other women recover from their husband's infidelities without needing to resort to tit-for-tat. Nowadays it's no great crime, is it? I'd told Oliver I had forgiven him. I *did* forgive him. I just felt so – second best. Unfeminine. I know I was wrong to have an affair. But I'll always be glad it was with Christos. If it had to be anyone, at least it was Christos. And at the time . . .'

She gives a drawn-out sigh. She is sapped, looks gaunt and exhausted. At the time. And so many happenings since, to erase that time.

4

'Lots of kids here wet their beds,' Maria says, threading a shell necklace while lying on the big sofa and Gnat sits on the arm.

The TV's on and Jason and Pete are glued to it. Pete is a new arrival who vandalised his own home because nothing ever happened there. Lisa is waiting for her father to visit; her real father who visits every month, turns up in an old Mercedes with a toy nodding dog at the back and dangly things hanging from the mirror in the front. He stays about five awkward, dutiful minutes then roars off in his car, almost leaving skid marks in the drive in his eagerness to be gone.

'What about your mother?' Gnat asked her.

'She walked out when I was four. That's why I was fostered.'

Maria goes on, 'I don't know why you should be so fazed about a bit of pee. Everything's different here. Nothing matters, does it? You can't get embarrassed anymore. There's no pride in you left to be embarrassed.'

Her feet are encased in bandages. Two days earlier she smashed her drinking glass to the floor and, before anyone could prevent her, trampled barefoot upon the shards. Gnat looked on in horror, cannot reconcile the soft-voiced, Madonna-faced girl with the person who committed that act

• Valerie Blumenthal

of self-violence. It has made her feel aloof towards Maria, this proof of her madness.

She can't stand blood; turns away during the gory parts of films. And the evening with her mother haunts her.

I'm not sorry.

But the blood was another thing.

Almost a month. She has been here almost a month and is sometimes overwhelmed by a feeling of claustrophobia which worsens as the day wears on. It commences as a mild itching in the neck and becomes a great cloud fuzzing around her, until she must run from wherever she is and inhale voraciously. She always seems to be running.

Summer air, stifling and freak-hot after the rain. The leaves, the grass are lush. But she is arid. This place is arid. And loopy. This morning she went to reclaim a pair of knickers she had washed and hung to dry over the window ledge. Cheryl had got there first and, laughing, pushed them off the edge. They fluttered to the ground, into the path of a boy who picked them up, sniffed them and danced off with them. The two girls gaped in amazement.

'Balmy. Everyone's balmy,' sighed Cheryl.

'Speak for yourself,' retorted Gnat.

'Well at least *I* know when I'm going home,' the girl said pointedly. 'A week today in fact.'

Gnat hasn't a clue when she'll go home. It seems a daunting and unlikely prospect, and she has yet to have that first meeting with her mother. It has been arranged for Tuesday, in four days' time.

That day, during breaktime, in front of everyone, there is one of those sudden flare-ups.

'You lay off him,' Janine threatens Cheryl in her low growl. 'Hear that? He's mine.' While John, the hulking object of their mutual desire, smirks a few feet away.

'He can make his own choice, can't he?' taunts Cheryl, small and poutingly pretty compared to big Janine, despite the brace on her teeth. 'Can't you, John?' she calls, turning to him. 'What are the odds, everyone—' and turns back to Janine.

A flash. A small penknife blade thrust deep into Cheryl's neck and all the kids shrieking and scattering. From the various buildings appear members of staff. Gnat, rooted to the spot, stands with her mouth wide as the blood spurts from her friend's neck. Someone stifles it with a cloth. Janine being led away, ranting. Gnat being led away, hyperventilating.

'It's all right. It's all right.' The Spoon's arm around her.

'It's not. It's not. It's not all right.'

Much later that afternoon she escapes Maria with her bandaged feet and Lisa with her pathetic expectant face stuck to the window, and takes a fold-up chair onto the terrace, positioning it in line with the sun, near a small rockery from where come the sounds of wasps humming. Closing her eyes she can feel the sun burning her lids, penetrating them so that her head is filled with colour; like looking through one of those children's cardboard telescopes given away at the end of parties. And she wishes she were that age again, wishes everything could be as it used to. She becomes unbearably hot, lying there in her too-tight shorts, with the sun permeating her skin. Memories and thoughts are juxtaposed and iridescent spots prance behind the shutters of her eyes. She has a sudden longing for physical contact; the need to be embraced by another human being. The noises around her come from the depths of a well and she feels as though she has been pumped full of air and is floating. All she is conscious of is the lightness of her body and her isolation. A bell rings; distant. Perhaps she imagines it. Perhaps she imagines everything, even Turner's End. Perhaps she isn't here at all.

A voice says, 'Hey, Gnat – no tea?'

Her mouth doesn't move.

'Hey, why the tears?'

She had not been aware of them. She opens her eyes, jumps up from the chair and throws her arms around Dr Middleton. He strokes her hair. And the warmth, that wonderful warmth, not of the sun, but another caring person.

'I hate everything. I hate everything.'

'Want to tell me?' he asks her.

'Is Cheryl dead?' she says against his blue shirt.

'No. She's going to be OK.'

'Do you promise?'

'I promise.'

'I'm scared of dying,' she blurts out. 'I felt like I was dying, lying there.'

'What was it like? Can you describe the feeling?'

She wonders how to define it, stares at the Surrey hill and the white gravestones. 'Lonely. I mean really lonely.'

She looks at him, frightened and he regards her thoughtfully.

'There's no need to feel lonely,' he says. 'You're not alone, Gnat.'

She goes in to tea, with the unchanging plates of curled-up bread, and slides into the empty seat between Janine and Robert, ignoring Janine. She smiles at him. She understands what it's like to be locked within one's own silent world when the body becomes a cave that both imprisons and offers a refuge. After her father had died she had been locked in such a cave. She has a desire to lay her hand on Robert's and to place her lips chastely on his full ones. His blank, immutable expression deters her from kissing him, but in full view of everyone else she touches his hand resting on the table. She can see a muscle working in his cheek and is oblivious to the others watching curiously.

'Robert?'

He looks at her as though puzzled, and for an instant it

seems he would reach out to touch her cheek – and then his features crumple.

'No,' he shouts, leaping up from the table. 'Leave me alo-o-o-ne.' And he stumbles from the room, pursued by a nurse.

The spell is broken. 'I'm sorry,' Gnat yells, stricken. 'I didn't mean to do anything. I didn't mean to upset him.' And she too dashes from the room.

The Spoon catches up with her on the landing and hugs her.

'Gnat, he spoke,' she cries. 'Do you realise? You got him to *speak*.'

And then Gnat is laughing with her, waltzing with her down the passageway. She got Robert to speak.

That night she has trouble sleeping. The day has been too momentous: first the episode with Cheryl and Janine, then the dying feeling, and then Robert speaking. She doesn't wet her bed that night.

Pirate slept on her bed. His bean-bag was in the hall but half way through the night he slunk up to her room, nosed open the door which was always ajar in readiness, and sprang onto her bed where he lay with his head resting on the hump of her body. He snored in his sleep: human-type snores reverberating through her chest; sometimes he squeaked and whistled. She wondered what he dreamed of. The garden was like a mortuary with bones scattered about, and the gap in the fence enabled him to steal from the dog next door and add to his collection. Once he slithered through with a complete skewered chicken ready for the barbecue. Gnat thought he must dream of bones, as she listened to him squeaking. In the early mornings she studied him; his eyelashes beneath the slits of his closed eyes – old, white lashes, separated like minute diamonds.

• Valerie Blumenthal

He died when he was ten and she nine. His love of bones was his downfall.

'It happened outside our house,' Gnat tells Dr Middleton. 'Dimple had just arrived and the front door was still open. Everyone was chatting in the hall. Opposite they had a soppy Pekinese Pirate couldn't stand, although he never hurt it. He never hurt anything. Once a dying fly crawled in front of him while he was resting and all he did was push it ever so gently along with his nose. I forgot to tell you, he sang. Whenever I practised my cello he sang. Really sang. Lifted his head and yowled. Anyway, that day he had his hackles up and was growling at the dog on the opposite side of the road, but nobody took any notice. I mean he was much too sensible to do anything. But then that soppy Pekinese started digging—' Her voice becomes quicker and higher '– It dug up a bone as big as itself, and that was too much for Pirate. He tore out of the house and across the road just as a car was overtaking another and going too fast to stop. It was so dreadful. Pirate yowled. I screamed. So did my mother. And there was a bang as the cars crashed.'

She gives a juddering sigh. He laces his hands and waits gently.

'The driver who'd hit Pirate carried him over. He was – Pirate was – covered in blood. Daddy tried to make me go away but I wouldn't. I yelled at the man. I hit him, and my mother had to yank me away. She was crying too. Pirate was still alive, whimpering, and he tried to wag his tail. That nearly killed me. I mean he was so brave. Can you imagine – wagging his tail? He licked me too, from Daddy's arms. Despite everything he could still lick. Daddy cradled him while my mother phoned the vet. I mean it was awful, awful, and Dimple was just standing there, and I turned on her, because if she hadn't come the door wouldn't have been open.'

The vet arrived after Pirate had died, and he took the body

away in a sack. She couldn't believe that, her dog being carried away like a robber's bounty. Her father looked helpless and drained, and she noticed him clutching his stomach as though he had a pain; has a clear mental picture of him holding his poor tummy and no one bothering.

For several weeks she slept with Pirate's doggy-smelling bean-bag on her bed.

A year passed and with the tragedy of her dog slipping into the recesses of childhood, the pattern of things followed its usual course. Some sort of transition had taken place between her parents, invisibly drawing them closer. She can still see them vividly: together, welded together as never before. Their love for each other was transparent, and threatening to her; she was unable to penetrate their barrier and was jealous of their private exchanged glances.

Her parents. Her father, who had cancer.

• • •

The sixth principal event of her adult life.

Harriet had never known such a wanton, heady and carnal relationship as she had with Christos. She had never met anyone like him before. Everyone she knew was so respectable. She was so respectable.

She recalls the first time she went to her lover's flat – his father's flat; but he was always abroad.

'Do you work on the floor?' she teased as she surveyed the notes, books, files and journal cuttings strewn about so that one had to tiptoe between it all, seeking the odd spaces like stepping-stones. It transported her back to her own student days and she felt sadly old, wondered what she was doing here.

'Isn't the floor the best place?' he answered.

'I don't know how you bear it.'

'Believe me, everything's in order. Look –' And he picked up a wad of papers. '– All clipped together. Everything I need pertaining to chapter seven is here. And the relevant reference books are beside it. The cuttings too. The same applies to the other chapters. See? All in order, and even colour-coded for instant recognition! I need space on my desk for the actual writing.'

'You write longhand?' she asked, standing a little shyly by the desk, a stranger in his domain.

'Of course I do,' he said scathingly. 'Evolution gave me a thumb and fingers. I need the action of writing to make me think.'

'What happens to all this mess when your father comes back?'

'Oh he'll be gone at least six months. I'll worry about it then.'

She learned about mythology from him; about Nemesis, the goddess of retribution and daughter of Erebus and Night. The novel he was working on had as its heroine a modern-day Nemesis.

'There is some dispute whether Nemesis was in fact the daughter of Zeus and Necessity, but for my purposes I prefer Erebus and Night. More sinister and decadent,' he told her, looking directly at her, stepping adroitly over papers to be by her side.

She felt herself weakening. 'Who was Erebus?'

'Erebus was the son of Chaos and brother of Night. Erebus represents darkness. Erebus was also the region between Upper Earth and Hades.'

He ran his fingers up and down hers and his eyes foraged into hers.

'Hades?' she whispered.

'The underworld,' he whispered back, now running his hands along her shoulders, playfully licking her neck. She could smell his clean-hair smell and the freshness of his skin.

'The abode of the dead, guarded by the three-headed dog, Cerberus.'

She was aroused and wet. 'If Erebus was brother to night, and Nemesis—'

'Yes, incest. Do you disapprove?'

And he kissed her; a kiss of great sweetness, his lips soft and moist, his tongue in her mouth circling and making love to her. And she felt herself becoming more and more drenched between her legs, was slightly ashamed. It was years since she had been like this. Had she ever been like it?

In contrast to the sitting room the bedroom was immaculate; and austere. A tribal head-dress fixed to the wall presided over the bed.

'A Highland warrior's from Papua New Guinea,' he said as he gently pushed her, naked onto the bed, and kissed her upwards from the toes, kissed away her self-consciousness, her doubts about her narrow bony hips and tiny breasts, and small crease around her navel.

He lingered over her golden-toned body which was almost insane with longing for him to be inside her, left not a particle of her untouched. His fingers, sensitive as moth's wings, glided, massaged and probed; his tongue caressed. Beside herself with pleasure, she whimpered and trailed her nails along his skin. Smooth young skin. Their mouths were leeches clinging to each other. Finally he was edging his way into her: tantalising, light stabs; and then he was properly, deeply in her and she was surrounding him in relief, screeching out her relief; laughed afterwards that the whole of Windsor must have heard her.

She returned home that afternoon with an extraordinary sense of unreality, a detachedness from everything in the house. She was lightheaded and euphoric, could still feel Christos inside her. She fetched Natasha from school and was better able to withstand the hurt when the girl was stiff in her embrace. Strange child with her disjointed conversation and her immense cello she carted about. Sometimes she stared at Harriet in a way which made her wither.

Christos asked her about her daughter and she tried to change the subject. 'Why won't you tell me about your child?' he said.

'You're my child,' she replied, cradling his head.

He ducked angrily. 'I detest it when you're patronising.'

'That's your favourite word,' she teased.

'Well you are.'

'I'm sorry,' she said, contrite. 'Really I am.'

He immediately laid his head against her again. 'You never speak about yourself. I wish you would. You're so – mysterious.'

And at that she burst out laughing.

'Why, what's funny?'

'I'm the least mysterious woman in the world.'

Late spring, and she sat pillion behind him on his motorbike and rode out of town with him; saw someone she knew. But who would recognise her, an ordinary doctor's wife, wearing a helmet, on the back of a motorbike and with a Cambridge drop-out whose pony-tail streamed in the wind?

At first she was terrified, and then she felt the unravelling of her tension, the freeing of her soul, and she clung to him elatedly, as the wind stung her cheeks and they were speed itself as they tore through suburbs and countryside.

'All right?' he shouted.

'Very,' she shouted back.

'I love you,' he called out.

She could not say it in return. For the duration of their relationship she never said it.

'Did you love him?' the psychiatrist asks.

'In a way. But of course not like I did Oliver. It was—'

How can she describe her relationship with Christos? The

abandon and delight, the escapism, the tenderness, the irresponsibility, the way he fulfilled so many needs in her?

At the country pub where they stopped that day, Christos insisted on paying for her lunch.

'Listen,' he told her when she protested, 'I make enough with tips alone to afford a couple of pub lunches. Please, don't keep belittling me.'

He rarely alluded to his job in the wine bar; it genuinely pained him. He believed passionately in himself as a writer and she had to admire him for that.

'I'm going to rent a cottage in Suffolk,' he said suddenly. 'Come and live with me.'

'Don't be silly,' she answered, lightly pulling his pony-tail which did not look absurd on him.

'I'm serious. With your daughter, of course.'

'It's impossible. You know it is,' she said.

'You're such an exciting woman,' he told her.' Just being with you makes me happy. Did you know you had that ability? Serendipity? The first thing I noticed about you was your eyes – chestnut eyes. I thought that behind them dwelled a very lovely woman.'

A lump came to her throat. 'That is the sweetest thing anyone has ever said to me,' she said, turning away so that he wouldn't see the wetness in her eyes, pretending to search in her bag for something.

The house was untidy and it didn't matter. She disregarded Natasha's toys littered throughout the place. She felt reckless and exultant, and even as she walked about the house she was conscious of her body and its womanliness. She thought of Caroline Anderson. C. Christos would also be C.; and if Harriet kept an appointment book Oliver would find C. liberally scattered about in it. An agent and a writer. For the first time the literary connection struck her.

One-upmanship, Astrid called it.

Sorting Oliver's socks for the wash, looking at them,

scrunched up from wear, she imagined his feet – square, short feet – in them. His feet, his socks, endeared him to her and she was filled with compassion. She knew that the softening process had begun.

'You're the first woman I've ever loved,' Christos told her one summer afternoon while they lay, spent, on his dishevelled bed.

'How many can you be expected to have loved at twenty-four?' she answered. Sometimes when she thought of his youth she hurt within herself.

For his birthday the previous week she had given him a pastel drawing she had done of a couple embracing, naked, by a window.

Now Christos went to stand by the open window, smoking broodingly. 'There, you're doing it again,' he said, his back to her. 'Belittling what I feel.'

'But I wasn't.' She shook her head vigorously. 'Not this time. You misunderstood me.' She thought that he didn't know her and it was her fault; that no one really knew her; that once Oliver had.

She joined Christos and leaned her head against his shoulder. She was almost as tall as him. And there they were, the protagonists from her own drawing: embracing, naked by the window with the curtain puffing in and out.

She smiles wistfully in the psychiatrist's neutral-toned room, remembering that other room seven years ago. Not long, seven years, and yet what changes, what events have been enacted in that time.

He asks, 'When Christos told you you were the first woman he'd loved did that give you a sense of power?'

'No, nothing like that. When he said it I felt—' She tries to conjure up old emotions since replaced. 'I think I felt privileged. And I think I was worried for him because I couldn't give in return. I knew nothing could come of the relationship.'

'Had he been older would you have contemplated going to live with him?'

'But it was partly because of his youth that I was drawn to him. I don't think I ever wanted to abandon my marriage. I'd never stopped loving Oliver.'

'You were using Christos then.'

'No!' she protests, standing up. 'No,' she repeats, re-assuming her usual quiet tone and sitting down again. 'It was a relationship of tenderness and mutual respect. It fulfilled different needs in each of us. So maybe we were both using each other.'

'Nevertheless, you were the one at the helm.'

She pulls a wry face and concedes: 'Yes.'

'Did you enjoy that?'

'I suppose it was something of a novelty for me. Yes, I suppose I did enjoy it, if I actually think about it.'

'It's understandable,' he says, blinking slowly. 'Under the circumstances. What about the physical side of your marriage during this period? Were you able to have sex with your husband?'

Harriet blushes, fearing she is about to blacken herself. 'I could compartmentalise things. It sounds awful, doesn't it?'

When he doesn't reply she takes this as disapproval and continues hastily, 'I had this secret I guarded to myself and it buoyed me, restored my own sense of worth. I had felt demeaned by Oliver, despite all he'd done to try and make reparation. I'd lost my confidence, my sense of – womanhood . . . I didn't like him for what he'd done to me . . . Oh God, I feel so dreadful saying that. You don't know how it hurts me. I only mean for a *while* I didn't . . . Oliver was my life . . . Oh God, I feel so disloyal . . .' Her tears gush and he waits respectfully for her to compose herself.

'What about Natasha during this time?'

'Nothing changed. Either Oliver or I took her to school. I always fetched her. I took her to the park, to the supermarket, shopping, tested her on homework, cooked her favourite things. Nothing I did made her love me, because she didn't want to, do you see? She *wanted* only to love Oliver. I was just in her way . . . I remember he had to go away for a weekend course—' she smiles faintly, 'genuinely this time. Natasha hid in a kitchen cupboard and refused to come out. When I pulled her she scratched me like a cat. Oh God, I did my best with her you know. I really did.'

She tugs the band from her hair and massages her head where the hair had been pulled tight and made it sore.

She recalls how after that quarrel with Natasha she wished she could flee the house, her husband, her child, damn all responsibilities, damn rows and hysterics and gloom and ingratitude, guilt and blame and anger; defy them all and – yes – run to Christos. And because Harriet is purging herself to this man she confides how nearly she was tempted.

'That's perfectly natural,' he tells her in his measured tone; and she could almost kiss him. 'The fact is you didn't go. Your sense of logic and responsibility prevailed. How long did the affair go on for?' He peers at her beneath his unruly brows.

'It lasted about four months. It ended—' Harriet rests her head against the back of her chair and closes her eyes. 'It ended when he had an accident. A frightful accident.'

She hadn't heard from him for three days and telephoned him. A woman's hoarse foreign voice answered, and Harriet was filled with foreboding as she asked to speak to Christos.

'I'm his mother. He's had an accident,' the woman said, weeping down the phone. 'With the motorcycle. His neck is broken.'

That youthful neck.

'Who are you?' His mother sounded demented with grief.

'A friend,' she replied numbly. 'I'm a friend.'

'Yes, but who *are* you?'

And who was she? She was not his girlfriend. She ignored the question and asked her own. 'Which hospital is he in?'

'The Royal Berkshire, in Reading. Who is this? Are you his woman?'

'Sort of. I'm sort of his woman. I'm sorry. Oh I'm so sorry about your son, about Christos.' Crying, she replaced the receiver.

She visited him that afternoon in the Royal Berkshire Hospital, quite forgetting it was Tuesday, her husband's fat-lady-day. His doctor jokes were, anyway, a thing of the past. And as in a vignette she kept seeing herself and Christos making love; his Apolline body which would never again know sensation. She saw them, the pair of them on his motorbike, carefree, immune to danger and mortality. It could have been her too.

It was only him: lying behind a screen in the ward, a network of tubes running around him, and bags containing fluid and draining fluid – just as once she had seen her father. An electronic graph at the foot of the bed monitored his heartbeat. His face was unmarked and waxpale, the rest of him covered by blankets. His eyes opened as she appeared round the screen.

'Christos?'

He attempted to smile. Her name came thickly and was unintelligible through barely parted lips. She kissed his forehead lightly, avoiding the tubes and bottles and bags, and tasted the salt of his eyes. And then a nurse told her she must leave.

'Your minute's up, I'm afraid,' she said.

She turned and looked at him before the screen was pulled across: a final glimpse of his marble face.

She blundered her way along the corridor, down other corridors, becoming hopelessly lost and not caring, too upset to ask anyone. Lost in a conglomerate of buildings linked by a maze of linoleum floors. And as chance would have it, she bumped into her husband.

Fat-lady-day. And her eyes streaming.

Reaching now for the Kleenex, remembering: the relief of seeing him, the utter joy of seeing him. And throwing herself sobbing into his astonished and comforting, such comforting arms.

5

'I didn't know what was wrong with him then of course,' Gnat says. 'Not at first anyway. I mean you don't think your father can die, do you? Sometimes I used to think about dying and I'd get frightened and I'd say my prayers extra hard at night. I'd imagine being an orphan until I'd cry just thinking about it. But I couldn't quite believe my thoughts, if you see what I mean. Daddy was there. He'd always be there.'

But she sensed something was seriously wrong. And in the darkness she whispered her secret fears to God: her father dying, earthquakes, murderers, her cello exam, wars – becoming more and more overwrought, and frightened that like a genie God might actually manifest himself before her. And sometimes she felt that the furniture was jeering at her as she muttered into the night; that the wardrobe, the chest of drawers bent double and rocked in mirth; and she slid down further under the duvet.

Then, when she was ten and her body developed prematurely and hinted at downy shadow in grown-up parts, she decided that God couldn't possibly hear everyone's thoughts or whispers all over the world.

'And as for Heaven,' Gnat says to Dr Middleton, 'how could there be room for us all up there? And what happens to all the insects and things? God must think we're all suckers or something. And if there's God, Daddy wouldn't have died. And what about wars? All those people praying to live but getting bumped off. No. There's nothing.'

Sorrow had invaded their house. It was in the hushed voices and tentative footsteps, in her mother's frightened-fawn eyes and in her father, melting in bed like in her dream.

She would go directly to his room after school and sit beside him. Propped against pillows, he would help with her homework and they would chat about her day. Sometimes he would doze off in the middle. He had had chemotherapy and most of his hair had fallen out. There were bald chunks interspersed with dark tufts.

Then came a spell when he seemed to rally. He got up, came once more to her room and played with the train set; listened to her cello practice. They walked by the river.

'My two women,' Oliver said, with Harriet one side of him and Gnat the other.

He was thin and stooped and in the street people stared, he looked so ill and odd. Gnat poked her tongue out at them when her parents weren't watching. Her father was game, so game to try anything. He took her rowing on the river, but after a quarter of an hour he'd had enough. He apologised. Once he attempted to mow the lawn. Gnat saw him from the window, wearing his crumpled farmer-Giles hat and plodding determinedly behind the machine. But after a few rows this, too, was abandoned. Another time he climbed the ladder to the attic.

'May I enter, Miss Edwards?' he asked as he had used to.

'You may, Dr Edwards,' she answered, happy, so happy to have him there.

Doctor. He must have known before his illness was diagnosed.

His respite was brief and illusionary, and once more he was confined to bed. Gnat incanted her nightly prayers;

in case. She fondled her sprouting body, intrigued and disgusted, and fell asleep with one hand between her legs and the other round her owl on the pillow.

Her mother was hollow-cheeked and distracted. Once she cooked pasta and added sugar instead of salt. On another occasion Gnat went to the fridge in search of satay sauce and found a bar of soap but no sauce. She discovered it upstairs in the bathroom where the soap should have been. Fleetingly she felt a wave of affection for her mother.

'You put the satay sauce in the soap tray,' she told Harriet, who was ironing in the breakfast room.

'Did I?' Harriet glanced up, unsmiling.

Her vulnerability was not what her daughter wanted, and aggrieved, Gnat went up to her room. She took her cello and bow from the case and played a piece by Sarasati which suited her mood, sawing viciously at the strings.

The doctor – a family friend – came and went; Dimple lent Gnat her favourite horse book; at school the teachers were lenient. She provoked them deliberately, but their patience suddenly knew no bounds. All these things compounded her suspicions.

One afternoon when she returned from school, Gnat as usual went directly to see her father. He held his arms open feebly from the bed: a wasted, completely bald and unrecognisable man. She snuggled against him and smelled his clean pyjamas fresh from the airing cupboard combined with his stale flesh.

After a while, when they had discussed her day, he said, 'Gnat, you know I'm not very well, don't you?'

'Yes I know,' she said, feeling a shivering within her, and nestling into his skinny warmth.

'Are you a brave girl, darling?'

'Yes.'

His tone filled her with dread. Vividly she remembers that dread.

'I've got to go into hospital. To stay there for a while. Not just for my treatments.'

'Why have you?' she shrilled. 'I won't let you. I'm coming with you.'

He laughed then. How could he laugh?

'When are you going?' she asked, clutching his shoulder.

'In the morning.' He held her hand, squeezing and kneading it.

She knew. At last she knew for certain. It was agony, the knowledge. She cried and cried, as she is now, thinking about it. Then she thinks of Pirate. Then her mother. And Dimple. Her mother again. Snapshots whisked away from her. It is as though she is twirling a hoola-hoop round her and it won't stop. It rotates madly in a blur of colour and fragmented faces. Life is a hoola-hoop.

... Her father fingered her hair, played with a curl. 'You've got such nice hair haven't you? So soft and fluffy. Little Gnat,' he murmured.

'You're not going to die. I won't let you. I won't let you die,' she sobbed, clutching him, his fragile bones in the pyjamas.

She had spoken the word and he said nothing to contradict it. He continued to play with her hair without speaking at all. And the following morning he did go into hospital, and he could die. He did die.

'At home in the summer there always seem to be thunderflies in the bath. My mother puts oil in it and they stick to the sides. It must be grisly ending up as a black smear on a Kleenex.'

'Really grisly,' Dr Middleton agrees, amused.

Gnat continues, 'I rescued a dying wasp once and it stung me. It was drowning in the river. So much for gratitude.'

'Do you like insects?'

'Not particularly.'

'Yet you rescue wasps.'

'I don't like dead things. Death. It frightens me.'

'Gnat, let me ask you something. Are you able to link your own action of a few weeks ago with death?'

She lifts her finger to fiddle with her stud, forgetting it is missing. 'No, I suppose not.'

He persists, 'Do you think you could do the same again?'

He has made a steeple with his hands and she remembers herself and Dimple in the school playground playing, 'Here's the church, here's the steeple.'

'Gnat?' the psychiatrist prompts her gently.

She can't bring herself to contemplate that evening and shouts at him, 'Why must you always bring it up?'

But she doesn't take flight as once she would have, and he repeats the question.

She slumps back in her chair and gazes at the ceiling. 'No,' she whispers into its greyness.

Silence, a strange weightless silence pervades the room and surrounds her. It seems to last for minutes. For the first time she notices the photographs on Dr Middleton's desk: a woman and a little boy. Were they always there?

'Are you married?'

'Yes.'

'Oh.'

'I have your permission?' he teases.

But she is too disappointed to laugh.

'Why are you so afraid of death, Gnat?'

'It's not being here. It's horried. Just not to be here.'

'You weren't here before you were born.'

'That's different. I didn't know anything then.'

'You don't once you're dead either.'

'Yes, but I've known it all once, haven't I? I mean I don't want it to suddenly end and – nothing.'

'You keep saying there's nothing. You can't know that for certain.'

'Daddy died, didn't he?'

'That doesn't mean his soul hasn't gone somewhere else.'

'Well anyway, he's gone.'

'Yes I know. And so might have your mother.'

'But she didn't. Only he did.'

Why does he always make her cry? Yet she has come to look forward to these sessions and to depend on this man. She actually likes crying here, in this room which is awash with youthful tears.

'So you believe your mother should have died instead,' Dr Middleton remarks pleasantly, and Gnat stops crying abruptly, shocked.

He stands up. 'Enough for now,' he says, helping her to her feet.

'I'm always blubbing,' she mumbles, rubbing her running nose along her bare arm, leaving a silver line on it like a slug's trail.

'That's a good thing.'

'Why?'

'You have to recognise your unhappiness before you can be happy,' he tells her.

So you believe your mother should have died instead.

The sentence, the casual way he uttered it, rings in her head. In the hallway she finds it hard to breathe. She sees The Spoon and, forcing herself to sound offhand, asks for some money.

'What for, Pet?'

Since the 'Robert' incident a rapport has grown between them and the nurse has taken to using this nickname. She must have been lying in the sun, for her face is a mass of freckles, and the skin between them, pink.

'Some new mascara,' Gnat says, trying to breathe normally.

'Is £1.50 enough?'

She hesitates, nods, and is off, into the August sun, her

little brown legs quick. Her frayed denim shorts cling to her bottom, her white tee-shirt with its black 'Bad-Girl' motif slips off one shoulder. She lets it: it's the look. A truck driver swivels his head and whistles as she walks up the hill and she gives him a 'V' sign and yells, 'Dirty old man.'

Tom's complexion is the tan of her old school shoes. By contrast his hair is white cotton wool. The rocking horse is finished and Tom is working on a bookcase.

'Ah, my favourite assistant's arrived,' he greets her. 'Plug the kettle in and make us both some tea, there's a good lass.'

This is always her first task, and although she would prefer Coke she enjoys the ritual. She puts tea-bags in two stained mugs, adds a couple of sugars to his, then boiling water and powdered milk, stirring with a bent teaspoon caked with the residue from other cups of tea. Her lips ground together in concentration, she shuffles through woodshavings and sawdust with the mugs, passes him his, and sits down on a tiny three-legged stool. An old milking stool, he said when she commented on it.

'Ta. So how's Gnat then?'

'All right. The same. It's boring, boring, boring.' Then she brightens. 'I got a boy to talk.' And she tells him about Robert, while Tom's trembling hands take three attempts to align the moulding onto the front of a shelf.

She has the sudden need to confide in him about Janine and Cheryl, to help exorcise the incident and also to see his reaction. Relate it to herself.

'A girl called Janine stabbed my friend Cheryl with a penknife the same day as I got Robert to talk.'

'Oh my, that can't have been very pleasant.' He stops what he's doing to look at her, and she gazes down at her trainers, dusty and beige, reminiscent of the sand and beach holidays.

'It wasn't. It was awful. Oh Tom, it was awful.' Gnat

shakes her head to dispel the images that follow her like her shadow. 'Janine went crazy. It was over this creepy guy, I mean really creepy, called John – she was jealous you see. And she'd got this penknife in her pocket nobody knew about and stabbed Cheryl with it in the neck.'

'Oh my,' Tom says again, very slowly. 'And you saw it happen?'

'Yes. There was blood all over the place.' No longer sure to what she's referring.

'Poor you. Poor you. And the lass. Is she all right?'

'Yes.'

'What about the other one. The one as did it?'

'What do you mean?'

'Where's she gone?'

'Oh she's still there. I mean if you're already in a loony place where do you go from there?'

He grinned. 'Well that's true I suppose.'

'Tom, do you think it's dreadful what she did, I mean really wicked?'

'Well it ain't exactly nice is it? But there again I daresay she's sad and mixed-up. She must be, mustn't she, to be where she is?' He's no longer looking at her, busying himself rather too deliberately with another piece of moulding.

'Oh Tom—' She so nearly tells him then, so wants him to like her as she really is, for being sad, not bad. But can't do it. 'Did your great-grandson like the rocking-horse?' she asks instead. 'Oh yes—' he grips a nail between his teeth as he speaks. 'Thrilled to bits he was. I lifted him onto it and explained what it was. He touched it all over. Such a clever little mite he is. Talks ever so grown-up. "I can see it in my head, Grandad," he says to me."' Chuckling, Tom removes the nail and hammers it lightly into the side of the bookcase.

'What did he mean, he could see it in his head?'

'Didn't I tell you? Little mite's blind. He were born like it.'

Tom takes noisy gulps of his tea, wiping his wet lips with the back of his hand.

Gnat thinks of Tom working away, lovingly crafting the horse, plugging the real hair mane tuft by tuft into minute holes along the crest of the neck; and the three-year-old child gleefully receiving a gift he can see only in his head. Yet he can have no concept of the precise meaning of 'see' any more than a deaf person can imagine sound. What does colour mean to him? She thinks of trees and grass; the countryside; green. Freedom. If freedom could be painted it would be green.

'It's so sad,' she says mournfully. The slightest thing stirs her emotions nowadays. She worries she's becoming wet.

Tom puts down the hammer. 'The little mite's happy, believe me. He doesn't know no different. His mum dotes on him. It's like that, isn't it? Lads and their mums, lassies and their dads. I expect you've got your dad wound round your little finger, have you?'

'He's dead,' she says.

'Ah,' Tom sighs, downing his tools again. 'Now that *is* sad. That's ever so sad.'

So you believe your mother should have died instead.

'My mother refuses to call me Gnat. She insists on calling me Natasha.'

'That's a pretty name. Natasha.'

'It's wet.'

'Now what might that mean?' he asks, perplexed.

'Wet. Uncool.'

'Dear me. And what does uncool mean?' He grins with cracked lips and reaches for the pipe lying across an ashtray and lights it, making small puffing sounds.

'It means drippy. Wet. Pathetic,' she explains.

'Well I never. Uncool. Wet. Well I never.' He draws pensively on his pipe. 'Well I think Natasha's much nicer than Nat. I agree with your mum.'

• Valerie Blumenthal

'It's Gnat with a G. though. Like the insect.'
'What do you want to be called after an insect for?'
She feels let down, disgruntled, and picking up a stanley knife, shaves an offcut of wood.
'Now you be careful of that, it's sharp,' Tom warns – too late as the blade slips down the wood and cuts into the webbed skin between her thumb and index finger. Blood flows.
She begins to scream and he tries to placate her.
'Hush, let me look. It's surface. Now settle down, there's a good lass.'
At the sink he holds her hand under the cold tap until the water runs pink and then clear, and meanwhile Gnat sobs quietly; broken-hearted sobs. Tom murmurs soothingly as he pats the cut with a towel and applies an elastoplast.
'I hate blood. I hate blood.'
'You wouldn't make a good murderer.' He laughs and snaps shut the first aid tin. 'I told you to be careful now, didn't I? But you're all tidy now, eh? Feeling better?'
'Yes.'
'What a to-do over a spot of blood.'
'I'm sorry,' she says, embarrassed, pushing some sawdust about with her feet.
'What for then? Silly mite. My girl were always doing things at your age. Got into ever so many scrapes. Drove her poor mum balmy. Funny to think she's a middle-aged woman now. It were all part of growing up I reckon. Learning to understand each other's needs. That's what life's about, if you think. Understanding one another. Give each other a bit of breathing space, I says, but show you care. Pass me the fine sandpaper will you? It's in the top drawer of the table.'
He puffs on his pipe, works away with his uncomplying fingers, wipes sweat from his forehead; and recounts a tale he has told her twice before. She has noticed he repeats

himself and wonders if he's going daft. It upsets her the way old people do; and she thinks of her grandfather, still as a rock in his chair. Everyone must think she's daft to be in Turner's End. Is she? Do those black rages, those moods of isolation, mean she's really loopy? At least she doesn't lick her plate at the table or drool like Jason, or believe herself to be a high priestess like Maria; or have a phobia about blue like Alice, or think the world's chasing you, like Susan. And she's never stolen anything or cheated in her life.

She says goodbye to Tom and is half way down the alleyway when suddenly she knows she can't go back to Turner's End, can't face the repetition of routine, the cheerful nurses and mixed-up kids. One big happy family – day after day after day, as though life begins and ends there and no world exists beyond its boundaries. And tomorrow afternoon her mother is coming.

So you believe your mother should have died instead.

Gnat waits at the bus stop, hugging herself to keep warm and rubbing her goose-pimpled arms and legs. Overhead the sky has clouded over and the air has chilled. Back at Turner's End they'll be in the middle of tea. The dried curled bread and thick, ivory coloured tea. But the caramel biscuits are nice.

No bus comes. The sun doesn't reappear. Her watch shows 4.40. An outsized watch whose strap is tangled with the string bracelet she herself made – dirty and discoloured now. And she toys with it, shifting from one foot to the other. Where will she go? Epsom? Brighton? The sea. Oh how she yearns for the sea. But she has £1.50. How will she get anywhere for that? And what would she do once she got there? How would she find a job? Perhaps she could pretend to be older. But where would she spend the night? And she is only wearing shorts. And her owl is at Turner's End. She is cold, feels conspicuous now in the overcast afternoon wearing her 'Bad-Girl' tee-shirt and tight shorts.

And someone would be bound to come searching for her. They'd tell the police; she would become a Missing Person.

She turns and trudges dispiritedly down the hill. So much for the big adventure. Gnat can't even run away. She's become wet.

'Fuck,' she swears out loud, breaking into a run. 'Fuck, fuck, fuck.' As she runs faster, all the way back to Turner's End so she won't miss tea.

• • •

Harriet climbs into the hired car. It will cost a fortune, she knows, but Elliot is away on business and she is too fraught to drive herself to Turner's End. She settles herself in the back, loosely supporting the cello which stands in its case on the floor.

'Blimey, Missus,' the driver says when he sees it. 'Whatever's that?'

'A cello.'

'Cor, you play that?'

'No, my daughter does.'

'Blimey, you don't look old enough to have a daughter who'd play a ruddy great thing like that.'

He prattles on for a while and she makes the appropriate comments at the right times; but he soon gathers she wants to be left in peace and reluctantly stops talking.

Harriets fantasises how it could be: her daughter is running into her arms and she rocks her as she did when Natasha was a baby, before she had a mind of her own. Her child, nestling in the crook of her arm. But of course it won't be like that. Instead they will grope for one another; founder and grope, and maybe they will find. Dear God, with all her heart she wishes for that.

* * *

Remembering: Natasha, wan and wasting, pining away for her father, not uttering a word for three weeks.

'Talk to me, darling. Darling, talk to me, please.'

And the zombie eyes looking vacantly back at her.

And when eventually the girl re-emerged into the world, she was changed; the aggression only hinted at before was now openly expressed. Harriet realised that her daughter hated her.

The car jerks to a halt at a pedestrian crossing, and Harriet herself jerks forward. The driver sees her in the mirror.

'Sorry about that. All right then, Missus?'

'Yes, fine thank you. I'm fine.'

'Mind if I smoke?'

'No, not at all.'

Oliver, who was vehemently anti-cigarettes, insisted that nobody was allowed to smoke in the house, and after Astrid visited Harriet would open all the windows wide so that her husband would not detect any smell.

'God, the house is cold,' he'd remark when he returned home.

Christos languidly smoking. Everything he did was languid. It was all part of the image he cultivated, as much for himself as others. She had read his first novel and understood very little of it, failed to comprehend its 'message', as he put it. 'It's so original,' she said afterwards to him, for want of anything better to say. 'I told you, didn't I?' he gloated, taking it as high – and justified – praise. 'Publishers are a load of bullshitters. Let's face it, James Joyce was misunderstood, and now he's an icon.'

Sometimes she wondered whether he was in fact brilliant or simply a quaint poseur. It was almost as if he had decided to play the role of one of his fictitious characters. Once he commented that his life would be beset by tragedy; and this may have been no lay prophecy but something he determined to make happen.

'You're part of my tragedy,' he told her. 'Inextricably bound up. But I'll be the orchestrator of my own fate.'

'Don't be so melodramatic,' she said, exasperated.

. . . Oliver, bewildered, leading her from the labyrinth of corridors, outside, into the haven of his car.

'What are you doing here? Tell me what's happened?' he asked as she wept within the enclave of his arms.

She did not know how to start with her explanation. It was easier to cry.

While he drove her home he gripped her hand on his thigh and she could feel its warmth radiating through his trousers, the swell of his muscle. She sank back into the seat, musing over the improbabilities of circumstance and chance and the facility with which events could spiral and complicate a mundane existance. She thought of Christos lying paralysed. From now on if he wanted to blow his nose, another person would have to do it for him. If he had an itch, someone else would have to scratch it.

At home Oliver poured her a brandy.

'My car's still in the hospital car park,' she said.

'It doesn't matter, we'll fetch it tomorrow. What about Gnat?'

'She's going straight to Dimple's for the night.'

This normal little exchange seemed incongruous to her and had a calming effect on her; she gave him a small, sheepish smile.

Oliver's arm was around her. 'Are you going to tell me what happened?' he asked in his most gentle voice, the one which had seduced, wooed and wed her. And she thought that if only he'd always spoken to her like that none of this would have happened.

'I don't know how to.'

'Try. I've got wide shoulders.'

This made her smile again. 'You have. Lovely wide shoulders.'

'But you found others you preferred,' came his response, demolishing her smile.

'He's had an accident. He's broken his neck.'

The words spilled forth and the story of her affair was fed to him in breathless, out-of-sequence pieces. She stumbled her way through it, with a mixture of defensiveness, apologies and shame. Once she blamed him. Throughout, Oliver's arm remained solidly around her. His face was strained. He was sad rather than angry: for her, for himself, for themselves; generously, for Christos.

He poured her more brandy, tilting the glass to measure the amount. A precise man. He poured some for himself also and rejoined her on the sofa. In the early days they had made love on that sofa when they couldn't wait to go upstairs.

'You must visit him in hospital,' Oliver said. 'I know you must do that. Tell me – would the affair have gone on much longer?' He looked completely bemused. His short thick hair was awry from his ruffling it.

She hesitated. 'I don't think so. I think it had almost run its course.'

Without hurting him any more than he already was, how could she explain the special nature of her relationship with Christos? Yet, not to, cast it in a sordid light. She was exhausted, beginning to feel numb with her exhaustion.

'Quid pro quo,' he muttered. Then, 'Oh God, oh God, oh God.'

'I'm sorry.'

He shrugged. 'I guessed almost from the start.'

'I thought you might.' She hung her head at the admission.

'You mean you half hoped I might.'

'Yes.'

'Retribution.'

Nemesis.

He removed his tie and undid the top button of his shirt,

and they sat without speaking for a few moments, both preoccupied with their thoughts.

'Do we stand a chance together do you think?' he asked her eventually, sounding like an uncertain boy.

'Yes,' she whispered, her throat aching with the love for him which had never left. And she saw Christos retreating down one of the corridors: her lover and her son, marble pale. What were his thoughts as he was catapulted from his motorbike? Was there a split second's exultation before fear? She felt as though she had killed him. You're part of my tragedy. And she had mocked him.

Oliver stretched out on the sofa while she continued to sit, heavily slumped.

'Lie down with me,' he entreated her. 'Nothing more. Please. I need to be close. I know I've sometimes been insensitive towards you. I haven't taken enough trouble to understand you. I want to understand.'

Cautiously she positioned herself alongside him. Their feet dangled over the end of the sofa. He held her.

'It's so hard,' he said. 'Thinking of you with someone else.'

His shoulders were heaving, and tenderly she wiped away his tears.

The hired car stops at traffic lights and Harriet stares through the window at the dismal row of red-brick shops. Outside his greengrocery store a rotund Asian man is buffing the apples, each one, so that its impossible redness is a beacon; and he replaces it in its crate amidst the other crates displaying their vivid contents. He pulls a handkerchief from his pocket and mops his brow, shiny beneath his heavy turban – and then the lights change and they are off. The little man's image remains with her; he had appeared so content buffing his apples in that disheartening place.

The built-up area gives way to trim Surrey countryside

with its rhododendron hedges and black-green pine trees creating shadows on the road surface.

'Nearly there then, Missus.'

'Yes,' she echoes, gripping the cello. 'Nearly there.'

6

In the reception Harriet picks up an ancient *Good Housekeeping* from a pile of magazines lying on the table and reads the same line three times about how to dry hydrangeas. Suddenly her bowels are weak and she bounds up from her seat and rushes to the lavatory. Washing her hands afterwards, she is confronted by her angular, troubled self in the mirror above the basin. She reapplies kohl pencil under her eyes and examines the fine lines fanning out from the corners, touching them ruefully. Never will she forget her fortieth birthday. That was the evening it happened.

Are there other mothers who are afraid of their thirteen- and-eleven-month-old daughters? she wonders, staring at her so-serious reflection.

Back in the reception Nurse Spooner is waiting for her, wearing her habitual, pleasant smile; and hoisting up the cello, her bowels weak again, Harriet follows her to the consulting room. The nurse presses Harriet's wrist encouragingly and knocks on the door.

'Come in,' a man calls, and with trepidation, Harriet enters on her own.

Dr Middleton comes forward to grasp her hand, but rudely she disregards him, stunned by the sight of the huddled figure of her daughter in a chair by the window, her face averted.

At this first glimpse Harriet is overwhelmed with relief. Maternal love courses through her. How could she be intimidated by this waif-like child with the soft curls, short brown legs splayed in front of her, and her feet bare. This is *her* child.

Propping the cello against the wall, she goes over to Gnat, who hasn't moved from her hunched position. She is almost bursting with her longing to touch the bent head and enfold her daughter in an embrace, as though their years of friction and wrangling never happened and that evening was a figment of her mind. Instead she must restrain herself, and she stands there uncertainly, looking down with brimming eyes, arms redundant at her sides.

'Natasha?'

In her apprehension the name bursts from her, not with the tenderness she feels but a stiffness she herself can hear.

'How are you?' she adds, listening with dismay to her crisp tone, her own mother's crisp upper-class tone; yearning to gather her child to her.

She glances in Dr Middleton's direction for help, but he has become the interested bystander and offers none, and she turns once more to the girl.

'I've brought your cello,' she says softly. 'It's got new strings.'

At last Gnat looks up, and the first thing Harriet notices is that the stud's missing from her nose, the second, her mutinous expression; and she shrinks back, feeling a crashing sensation within her. Nothing has changed. Her hopes plunge and her earlier impulses wither.

'I don't want it,' Gnat retorts sullenly.

And Harriet wants to cry out, 'You ungrateful little bitch.' She thinks about the silver charm bracelet, the care with which she chose the charms; the little dog with the ball. What has she done to this girl to make her want to inflict such hurt in return?

She shoots a beseeching look again at Dr Middleton, but his whole manner is impassive and she feels a wave of antagonism towards him, seeing him as a voyeur on their privacy. She continues to hover before her glowering daughter, until the psychiatrist suggests she might like to sit down, and she takes the vacant chair next to Gnat, deliberately placing her hands so that they appear loose and relaxed in her lap. She is conscious of her every action.

Dr Middleton studies first one of them then the other, as though they are a rare species. Gnat picks at a hangnail, while Harriet, fighting nausea, fighting diarrhoea, fighting tears, stares at her, then Dr Middleton, then out of the window, at two boys on the tennis court kicking a football over the net. Several minutes pass. Who's waiting for whom? Unbeknown to them, Gnat is sitting in a puddle in her chair, her bottom sticking to the wet plastic.

No longer able to stand the silence, Harriet laughs nervously and says, 'Well someone's got to talk.'

'Perhaps you would like to, Mrs Edwards.'

'I'm not sure what to talk about.' She gives another tremulous laugh, running her fingers through her fringe.

'I find that interesting,' he comments disconcertingly. 'Surely there's plenty to say.'

'Yes I know,' she agrees quickly, anxious not to appear foolish or neurotic. 'But it's so difficult. I find it so difficult.'

She turns to Gnat – who is apparently fascinated by her watchstrap.

'It's all so sad. It's sad that everything should come to this.'

The ready tears flow, and Dr Middleton magics a clean handkerchief from his pocket and passes it over; and this small demonstration of humanity placates her.

'Natasha's never been like other children I know with their mothers. It was always her father. Of course, Oliver had great charisma—'

'Daddy was perfect,' Gnat chimes in.

'My father was too,' Harriet says gently to her. 'But I don't expect he *really* was. I tried to be a good mother to you. I tried to give you love—'

'Tried, Mrs Edwards?' Dr Middleton pounces on her like a prosecutor in court. 'You mean it didn't come naturally?'

'No I don't mean that,' she answers indignantly. 'I mean that Natasha refused to accept my love. She only ever wanted it from Oliver. From my husband.'

Gnat fiddles with the string round her wrist. Old anger burns inside her; she can feel the itching starting and wriggles her shoulders to combat it, her thighs squeaking against the sticky plastic seat.

'Were you jealous?' the psychiatrist asks Harriet.

'Yes,' she admits, acknowledging the truth learned in that other room. 'She tried to alienate me and I believed she did it deliberately. I was superfluous. Yes of course I was jealous that she loved him and not me. For God's sake, I'm her mother. Didn't it count for anything?' she asks desperately. 'It never felt like we were a proper family. She always prevented it. She continually rebuffed me. It was . . . It was cruel.'

Gnat, who has never before heard her mother air her grudges, casts her mind back to those times she and her father were alone together and Harriet appeared on the scene, how she regarded her presence as an intrusion.

'Were you aware when her preference for your husband began?'

Harriet tilts her head at an angle; thinks of two-year-old Natasha's screaming fits and herself, worn out, screaming back. Oliver never raised his voice. Was it then? she asks. Possibly, the psychiatrist answers. Or possibly it was a year later when she had expectations of her daughter, made demands of her: that she tidy her toys at the end of the day, remain quiet while her mother was on the phone, didn't crayon on the furniture.

'Were you reasonable in your expectations of her? If you reprimanded her for crayoning on furniture, did you give her her drawing book? If she tidied her toys, was there some little reward?'

Harriet only remembers the constant effort, the constant conflict and the guilt that she was a bad mother.

'I shouldn't have had to bribe her,' she defends herself. 'It shouldn't have been so complicated.'

Gnat recalls that period from another viewpoint. 'She just flung commands at me.'

'That's not true. You were three. How can you possibly remember?'

'I do. And one night you were bawling at Daddy outside my bedroom.'

'Oh God, I don't believe this.' Harriet is tempted to get up and leave. She cannot take this battering or envisage that things will ever improve. There are too many obstacles to be overcome. She wishes she could forget she has a daughter. At this moment it is honestly what she wishes. And what would their reaction be if she told them that?

'You see?' she challenges Dr Middleton. 'You see how she launches into me? What have I *done* to you, Natasha, to make you like this?'

He remains silent, as does Gnat, and after blowing her nose Harriet calms down.

'Daddy and I had a quarrel that night. Because you only heard me didn't mean he hadn't done or said things too. Husbands and wives do quarrel sometimes. It's perfectly normal.'

How simple to tell her daughter, 'I'd just discovered your father's affair.' But Oliver in death has become deified.

'Natasha,' she says wearily. 'a person can only do his or her best. I know I'm not perfect—'

'Oh you think you are. So bloody, fucking perfect,' Gnat shouts.

'I don't,' Harriet shouts in return. 'How on earth do you know what I think or feel?' She shakes her head so that her pony-tail dances from side to side, and doesn't see the girl's startled expression. She is distraught with her sense of malignment, and this time when there is a prolonged hiatus feels no inclination to fill it. It is left to Dr Middleton, who has been coolly surveying the two sparring contestants, to be the mediator and do so.

'I think we should try and be constructive,' he tells them. 'While you are accusing each other, recognise you are at least communicating. That's important. No understanding can be reached between two people without communication. And that means absolute honesty – to yourselves and each other.

'Let's go through one or two points. It is, as you must know, Mrs Edwards, common for daughters to be closer to their fathers than their mothers and sometimes this is taken to extremes. Irrespective of how loving the mother is the child won't respond and will seek every excuse to justify her antagonism. Also, because it's usually the woman who spends more time at home, the role of disciplinarian is often down to her. By contrast the father, already the archetype male hero, is now shown to be indulgent and easy-going. The child reaches out even more, and in turn, flattered, the father responds.

'From what I gather, Gnat, you were a hyperactive toddler who was mentally advanced. This is often perplexing and exhausting for the mother and all her maternal feelings are challenged and become confused. She may even come to dislike the child, but can't possibly admit this and so disguises it with an exaggerated display of affection. Still the child rejects her, sensing her own power, which of course is a heady thing at any age, let alone then, and still the mother suppresses her feelings. We are left with no honest communication between the pair and a state of impasse that can only deteriorate, leading to enormous resentment on both sides, where each individual feels misunderstood.'

He breaks off and looks at Harriet for confirmation and she nods wordlessly, captured by what he is saying.

He continues, 'Often what happens is that when the girl is about ten or eleven she starts to relate to the mother and distance herself from the father, and by the time she's reached puberty her affections are evened out. She may even be faintly embarrassed by her father. In your case, Gnat, this distancing couldn't happen as your father died. You've been marooned in time, so to speak.'

Gnat, loathing this discussion, squirms in her sticky chair, gnawing at her nails. She refuses to blub like her mother; refuses to give in to them. And Dr Middleton sounds as smug as though he's just discovered the earth is round, and her mother has her lit-up expression. They make her sick.

'What I'm trying to establish,' Dr Middleton says, 'is the *positive* emotion which existed between the pair of you prior to Dr Edwards' death, so that there is something on which to build. If we can accept we all have faults and that it's impossible to be the perfect parent, partner or child all the time, it remains for you both to start respecting each other as individuals of worth.'

Through the window Gnat watches the two boys on the tennis court. The one grabbing the football is Robert, dishevelled and laughing. She has to escape. Everything is tumbling in on her. And out of the blue, Tom's voice: 'It were all part of growing up . . . Learning to understand each other's needs. That's what life's all about.'

She hates grown-ups. They always conspire together. She wants to be with the boys outside. She wants to kick the ball as hard as she can, watch it arc high in the air, travel so far it reaches her hill to become a small dot on the horizon. She is that dot. Why did her mother have to come? She was beginning to feel better before she came.

She whirls round. '*I'm* an individual,' she cries, standing up, forgetting about the wet patch, which they immediately see. 'And my name's Gnat. I'm Gnat,' she shouts at her mother, just as she did when she was tiny. 'Why won't you ever call me Gnat?'

Harriet is back in that other consulting room with the cruising taxis, and pedestrians scurrying past; and she recalls that night with her husband when they lay on the sofa and she talked about her affair.

For the first time he spoke freely of his lonely childhood, the lack of love from his divorced parents who'd favoured his younger sister; boarding school at the age of six; how, as he grew up he found it easier to be with strangers with whom he could retain his privacy and remain aloof; how hard it was for him to love because it meant the dropping of his defences. His relationship with Caroline Anderson had been on an impersonal, superficial level, he realised later. He peeled back the onion layers of his character and talked for hours about things he had for years guarded to himself, and in that single evening Harriet came to know her husband better than in all their time together. At Christos's expense she felt that old plenitude seeping into her; it was a feeling like sunbathing.

'You've always held back about yourself in the past,' she said.

'I know. I couldn't help it. I find it difficult to give of myself. You're a natural giver.'

'I got tired of giving,' she said. 'I needed to be selfish for a bit.'

His arm tightened round her. 'Did you ever think of leaving me for Christos?'

'No. Only in the odd fit of pique. Not seriously.' Blocking

her mind from those impossibly beautiful, irresponsible times with her lover. 'I'll never denigrate what he and I have. Had ... God, what is it now? I'm sorry but I can't do that.'

'I wouldn't expect you to.'

She thought about the springboard effects of infidelity, how it caused love to be fragmented and each of those fragments was worth so little, their sum total valueless compared to that rare and frail article they had debased and replaced.

There were so many kinds of love, and in her heart she had only ever wanted one. She detested complications yet her life was full of them. Maybe she had been naive before. Was maturity necessarily accompanied by cynicism?

'I really want to try this time,' Oliver told her. 'I want our marriage to do more than just survive. I don't want us to lose touch again.'

'Neither do I.' She circled her neck sensuously, loving his fingers combing through her fine hair.

'Then if we don't want it we shan't let it happen.'

'You haven't once criticised me.'

'Look 'ee to thyself,' he said dryly.

'It was dreadful seeing him like that.'

Christos, surrounded by gadgets which kept him alive, intruded upon the new beginnings of happiness. When she had kissed his eyes she had tasted salt. She felt immeasurable sorrow for him and in some obscure way, as though she were to blame.

'He'll only ever be able to move his head.'

They lay still together and Oliver's breathing grew heavy. She wasn't sure if he was asleep.

'It started when Natasha was born,' Harriet murmured. And he shifted his position, so that for a second she thought he was annoyed.

But he said, 'When she's grown-up I want her to think

of her childhood and recall her parents in love, solidly together. That's how we're going to be. We're going to keep working at it.'

It was how it was. Harriet will be eternally grateful for those two and a half years, during which she came to regard themselves as twin ripples of a river flowing in the same direction. At dinner parties if they were separated at tables they would turn, as if by telepathy, to each other at precisely the same moment and exchange a wink and knowing smile.

Astrid observed, when the three of them relaxed in front of a fire after a Sunday lunch, 'You two give marriage a bad name.'

'What do you mean?' asked Oliver.

'You make it seem like a viable proposition.'

From overhead came the sounds of Gnat practising the cello; the same passage over and over until she perfected it; then on to the next.

'Such self-discipline,' marvelled Astrid.

'She's a perfectionist,' Oliver said. 'She won't compromise.'

Harriet was silent, thinking that it was this very aspect of Natasha's nature which made her so inflexible and obstreperous. She would not let go until she had what she wanted.

The only times the girl seemed to need her were when she was injured or ill. She remembers when Natasha burned her finger on the gas flame: her trusting navy gaze as her mother dressed the dirty singed finger, kissing it after it was encased in elastoplast. And another occasion: Natasha had chickenpox and Harriet, gratified to be wanted, traipsed upstairs with hot drinks and a damp flannel, and treats and stories.

One day in the car Harriet switched on the radio and heard an interviewer questioning a leading industrialist about his reaction to his success.

'I breathe, but I don't inhale,' the man replied.

His words chilled her; she applied them to her rekindled love affair with her husband as though pre-empting its brevity.

'I've been offered a partnership in Fulham,' Oliver told her that night. 'It would mean a lot more money. What do you think?'

Ironically, it was she who considered their daughter. 'What about school, her friends?'

He was dismissive. 'She has to change schools in a year or so anyway. Children are adaptable. Her friends can stay at weekends. What about you?'

'I'd be near Astrid,' she replied. 'And my parents,' she added, her heart sinking. She wondered if she would find another teaching job. She envisaged the pleasure of being able to go to galleries and exhibitions and concerts.

'I'd live in a hovel with you.'

'How about one in Parson's Green?' He parted her hair and kissed the small bone at the base of her neck while she stirred a sauce on the cooker.

And at that moment Gnat appeared, observing them briefly from the doorway with a frown, before running back upstairs to write in her lock-up diary.

Oliver's pains started. Or rather Harriet became aware of them because he could no longer hide them. In reality they had started several months earlier. They had invaded him, his liver, his bones.

The seventh principal event of her adult life.

'His face was grey,' she says at the precise minute the sun disappears behind a cloud and a dark amorphous patch is thrown across the carpet.

The psychiatrist regards her compassionately from beneath the umbrella of his brows, and she covers her eyes and mourns anew her husband's grey face and those two and a half ephemeral years.

• Valerie Blumenthal

• • •

Gnat has come upstairs to get away from them all. It was funny at first: Craig had got hold of some scissors and lopped off Susan's plait without her even realising. Then he began swinging it round and round like a lasso, taunting her, and the truth dawned. They all started laughing and throwing it to each other; poor Susan's plait with its bright yellow ribbon being tossed back and forth while she danced from foot to foot, howling in the middle of their witches' circle. Suddenly Gnat wanted no part of it.

'Stop it,' she shouted at them. 'Leave her alone.'

Nobody listened, but within minutes a nurse was on the scene. Gnat slunk away and took refuge in her cello. Loopy, loopy, loopy. They're all loopy.

The Spoon comes to remind her about her afternoon session with Dr Middleton and finds her perched splay-legged on the edge of her bed, playing her cello, lost in it, oblivious to Maria, Alice, Robert and Jason listening in the doorway, having followed the sounds upstairs. Gnat needs no music, has always been able to play from memory. Her teacher had been so strict that when she hadn't practised she feigned illness rather than risk his biting sarcasm – a scrawny-necked, elderly man whose darting head reminded her of a chicken as he sawed the bow back and forth across his cello.

Finally Gnat looks up, blinking and smiling almightily. She had forgotten what it was like to play the cello, to elicit haunting sounds from it; to make music. 'I'm out of practice,' she says apologetically, laying the instrument on the bed and twanging its strings in an embarrassed way.

The Spoon claps heartily and the others join in. Robert comes forward and slaps her on the back, leaving her spine tingling, and she blushes. Then she starts to laugh; laughter bubbling to her throat. Jason reaches out to pull her hair and, still laughing, she prises his fingers loose.

Downstairs Dr Middleton remarks, of her glowing face, 'You look happy.'

'I've been playing my cello.'

'I wish I could play an instrument. You're very fortunate. What made you pick the cello?'

'Daddy bought a cassette of Elgar's Cello Concerto with Jaqueline du Prè playing. When I heard it I didn't know what it was, but it was the most beautiful sound on earth. I remember when I heard those first bars, the way the cello swooped down. It blew my mind. Daddy had to play that bit over and over for me.'

'How old were you?'

'I was seven. For Christmas that year I was given a baby cello and started lessons. I took grade six a year and a half ago,' she says proudly – then adds, 'But I stopped playing.'

'Why, Gnat?'

'I don't know. Things.' She shrugs. 'It seemed a bit wet I guess.'

Being ragged at school about it. Dave, whom she had the hots for and nearly 'did it' with, saying she just liked big things between her legs. Gavin taunting her for being posh.

'Will you resume it now?'

She know that this question is laden, that by answering affirmatively she will be deciding on a particular path.

Remembering: her father sitting in her room listening to her play; performing in local youth concerts; her mother's huge grin from the front row as she collected the music cup, her father too ill to be present. Instead, her mother was proud of her. She reflects on the enormous pleasure she derives from her playing. Nothing compares to it. Not listening to the funky rap of Ice T, or the troubled ghost of Kurt Cobain of Nirvana blaring out at top volume from her ghetto blaster. Their posters are all round her room at home. When

• Valerie Blumenthal

Cobain shot himself she wept loudly and ostentatiously with the other girls in her class and later wrote a poem about him. It crosses her mind now she hadn't really cared that much, only that she thought she should. She thinks of deafening rock concerts and screaming, stamping kids; of Rave parties – wearing a micro-skirt and heavy makeup, sticking her breasts out and nonchalantly showing her false ID which claimed she was eighteen, to the bouncers at the door. And a single terrifying experience with Ecstacy when her body felt propelled by a herd of stampeding horses . . . Thinks of herself playing Bach's Arioso in the church at a recital to raise money for the bell tower. When she visited Dimple in Windsor she broke the padlock to get into that same church, changed all the name labels on the choir robes, and hid bibles, eking out her revenge on the place for continuing without her.

Until now she hasn't touched her cello in a year except to cut its strings.

She broods on the prospect of staying here for ever and ever, Amen, in Turner's End Adolescent home; answers Dr Middleton's question with the tiniest 'Yes,' while gazing at a worn spot on the grey carpet; and feels relief wash over her.

After a contemplative pause he says they are going to explore Positive Emotion, which makes her curious; their sessions have become a game in which the jigsaw segments of her life are lifted from their mis-matched positions and, after trial and error, resited.

'Gnat, do you perceive your mother as a good or bad person? Please be truthful. One doesn't necessarily like a person who is good or dislike one who's bad. I use the terms broadly, by the way.'

Instantly wary, she nibbles on her nails, unwilling to think of Harriet. Too late; Harriet has been conjured up.

Greeting her daughter after school: 'Have a look in your room, There's a surprise there.'

And on her bed, a pair of much coveted Doc Marten shoes.

Her mother defending her before the headmistress of her old school when the old bat catalogued Gnat's vices before expelling her. And years previously, telephoning another parent to complain that Gnat was being bullied by her child. Driving her to rock concerts. Sitting through the same PG film three times. Encouraging her to paint. Helping her to select library books. Harriet, who would do anything for anyone, however busy; weeping over her own father in that infernal chair day after day; laughing over the spaniel's antics; trying to scrub the engrained paint from her finger

'She's OK.'

'A good person?'

'OK. So, maybe she is. What of it? Look I hate all this.'

'A good mother?'

'I don't know. I guess so. I don't know. I don't think about it, do I? I mean it's not the sort of thing one thinks about.'

'And would you say you're a good daughter?'

She springs up. 'Look, what is this? The bloody inquisition? How do I know? I mean how the fuck would I know if I'm a good daughter?'

'But you do know, Gnat.'

She grumbles, 'I'm fed up of this dump,' and twirls round on her feet.

That morning one of the girls from another dorm stole everyone's personal possessions and hid them all over the place. Outside, Janine and Alice are playing tennis. Alice's shocking pink tights make her legs resemble boiled lobsters and for some reason remind Gnat of her own silver party shoes. She wonders how her mother could have permitted her to wear them the whole time then realises she had no option: she, Gnat, would have thrown a tantrum.

'Would you say you're a good daughter?' he repeats.

'Things get me het-up,' she says. 'I can't help it . . . No one will ever love me.'

There is one of those significant silences, during which she presumes she is supposed to mull over everything, then: 'Do you want to go home?' he asks. 'At some stage is that ultimately what you'd like?'

The question catches her completely unawares and she stares at him for a few seconds. She swallows. 'I don't know. I'm frightened of going home.' There. She's admitted it at last. She sits down again.

'Why?'

Swallows again: the panic rising like the sea whooshing inside her; the longing, longing to go home but the fear of leaving here where it's safe. How can she ever go back after what she did?

'I don't know. I mean, like you said to her two days ago, so much has happened, hasn't it? I mean where do you start?'

'*You* start by learning to like yourself – to give yourself goals, haul yourself up. You start by getting on with the business of living instead of dwelling on what hasn't been and what can't be. You learn to respond to the people who are there and not people who aren't. You must learn to go on to the next stage, whatever that is and be prepared to shoulder disappointment. And you have to build your confidence so that you are your own person, someone to be proud of. Self-esteem, Gnat. Just tell yourself, self-esteem.'

'Self-esteem,' she repeats, articulating the words with slow precision, beginning to smile, and feeling a surging within her – of what? happiness? optimism? Such solace from those two words: self-esteem.

At supper that evening she cuts up Jason's food for him. Robert is on her other side. Shy, handsome Robert, who presents her with four jumping beans, who talks with a stammer; and she waits patiently for him to finish his sentences. Who but for her wouldn't be talking at all.

7

'Hello, Natasha.'

'Hello.'

This is their second meeting, and Harriet, scarcely able to hide her pleasure that her daughter returned her greeting, sits down next to her.

It's too bloody much to expect her to call me Gnat, the girl broods. Even after last time she won't do it.

Almost seven weeks she's been here, and summer is drawing to an end. Incarcerated at Turner's End for nearly the entire summer.

Dr Middleton reminds Harriet of the chairman at a committee meeting introducing the first speaker. Today it's Gnat, and he asks her to describe her 'silent' period after her father's death.

'It's three years ago,' she protests. 'I mean how can I be expected to remember? It's like looking through a fog.'

She catches her mother's eye, but when Harriet smiles encouragingly, looks down.

'There was this haze around me . . .'

She existed in the bleak darkness of her own mind. Black-clad hooded figures like executioners flitted between other phantom figures. And interspersed with the fantasy was a dimly realised reality: her own pain; people coming and going, the ringing of the door bell or the telephone; low murmurings; sobbing. She lay in bed for hours or sat in a chair downstairs, as immobile as her grandfather. She was fed. Her mother fed her, begged her, 'Darling, talk to me.'

'So you remember that – my feeding you, trying to get you to speak?' Harriet asks eagerly.

'Yes.' Gnat disentangles a lock of her hair and winds it round her finger.

'I cuddled you a lot to try and get you to talk. Do – do you remember that?'

'I don't know,' Gnat mumbles, wriggling her shoulders, blocking out her mother's arms around her rocking her like a baby.

And Harriet, clutching at any sign of a thaw in her daughter, dares to permit the little flame of excitement just starting to flicker inside her: that whilst her daughter claims not to remember, at least the question didn't provoke one of those dreaded temper fits; dares hope that slowly, so slowly, the seeds of reparation are being sown.

Gnat's head sinks lower and lower as she recaptures that time: the bleakness, the disbelief, the swollen feeling of her heart. Into her knees she says, 'I don't remember anything really. I was just there. I didn't want to talk. There was no point. There was nothing to talk about, was there? I mean what was there left to care about?'

Me, shrieks her mother inwardly. Me. Your mother. I was there. Her excitement of just seconds ago is completely, cruelly, demolished, her slight optimism, shattered. And back floods the old anguish, now with full force, filling her head and filling her chest. She can't take this. She simply can't, can't take it.

Dr Middleton as referee, observing them edging at a snail's pace towards the tentative beginnings of a truce and then away again, notes Harriet's furiously set jaw and asks Gnat, 'Have you ever thought what it must have been like for your mother? Her husband died. Can you imagine what it was like?'

Something snaps within Harriet and she bursts out, almost choking over her words, her face twisted and livid, 'Of course not. She has no idea. How could she? She was too selfish, too wrapped up in her own little nasty self. It was always me, me, me. She just shouted until she got her own way...'

Out it comes: all that rage, masked for too long, the resentment she's had to suppress and which has rubbed away at a love tested to its limits so that at times it has become hatred. Out with it all, like water rushing through a collapsed dam; the torrent of her emotions; the accumulation of years.

And Gnat listens, staggered, her suntanned face blanching; and Dr Middleton, impartially; and Harriet, hearing herself, unable to prevent the tirade pouring from her lips until finally it is over, and there is an extraordinary lull in the room.

Suddenly she gets up and does what Gnat has done so many times: she dashes, sobbing, from the room, from the building; and into the car. She drives away from Turner's End.

Her daughter remains behind, stunned. 'Well, so that's that, isn't it?' she says to Dr Middleton. 'She hates me. I mean she really hates me.'

And her voice sounds shocked and lonely. She is a very small, fluffy creature, curled there in her chair.

• • •

'I don't know what came over me.'

'It had to be released,' the little man assures Harriet. 'It couldn't stay bottled up inside you.'

She says despondently, 'I've ruined everything.'

'You haven't, you know. I assure you you haven't. You've

held back far too much over the years. It's time for you both to face the issues even if it means inflicting hurt and being hurt.'

She gives a bitter laugh. 'There's been plenty of that already.'

He nods one of his sympathetic nods and she sighs deeply; it runs through her entire body. 'It's never, never going to go away, all this.'

'I think it will improve. I do believe that.'

'So I must have faith.'

'I think you should.'

He asks her about the early days of her widowhood.

A thirty-six-year-old widow. She looked up the word in the dictionary; it was only five from wife.

Astrid came to stay with her and took over. Natasha floated about, ghostlike, mute, closetted in her room for hours on end. And then one day Harriet went in to see her and found her clearing the cupboards of all her toys, dismantling her train set, throwing everything willy-nilly into dustbin bags.

'What are you doing?' she asked, horrified.

'Getting rid of the lot,' the girl answered, her first words for three weeks.

Her mother came towards her. 'You can't just chuck it all, darling.'

'I can, I can, I can,' she replied furiously, kicking the sack, ducking Harriet's embrace.

In the end everything went to Oxfam, along with Oliver's clothes; but Harriet kept selected examples of each item: a shirt, a suit, several pairs of socks, pants, tie, his old corduroys, three jumpers. The car boot was so full it barely shut, and at Oxfam they were agog with unthinking delight as she unburdened her boxes onto the floor.

'Goodness, someone's had a clear-out,' remarked the old

lady sweetly, exclaiming over the train-set, over Oliver's clothes.

He used to survey himself in the mirror in those clothes, but to this woman they had no history. The body they had fitted, the flesh they had encompassed were without identity. And soon someone else's body would leave its own imprint, its own odour. Harriet drove home unhappy and lonely, and the boot lid wasn't closed properly and clanged on its emptiness.

The house she had created and into which she and Oliver had breathed life, felt antagonistic. Harriet bolstered herself against her grief and faced winter. She knew she would never be happy again, that the agony which seared her bones would not pass; and she hankered, hankered for Oliver. She used his toothbrush and his comb, wore his socks and jumpers; and tasted his mouth, smelt his hair, his skin. And learned somehow to cope. Nothing more. Only to cope.

She remembers the time she bled the radiator in her room and hot water gushed out as she turned the key frantically, unable to comprehend why it wouldn't work, her thumb pressed in vain to the aperture, and towels everywhere. For twenty minutes she was stuck there, resigned to the entire house being flooded. She dared leave her position for a minute to phone the plumber and the tone rang and rang, while the geyser shot across her room. Then she saw it – like a rat-dropping – on the floor: it was the valve which had been forced out. Fumbling, she pushed it into the hole and turned the key. It worked.

She wept with relief and with aloneness. She wept for the bills and forms and mounds of paperwork that arrived in brown envelopes daily amongst the letters of condolences and Christmas cards. She didn't understand half of them. She didn't know what to tackle first. She wept for Oliver, for sharing talks with him, sex with him, cherishing with him;

and for all the years ahead which she couldn't contemplate and yet she was young. She wept for her father, and over her daughter who had become a monster. She didn't cry again until she met Elliot.

And then, after the respectable first few months, when somehow she had survived winter, she found herself continuously running to answer the telephone. It seemed that every male, married or unmarried, wanted to test her availability, to try the new fruit left ripening by itself and perhaps over-ripening if not attended to. She had not realised she knew so many men, and was appalled by their lack of insight into the female psyche, that, as far as they were concerned, by virtue of her aloneness she was inadvertently offering herself and her wares as provocatively as had she stood on their doorsteps with her knickers down. She was astounded by their male arrogance and gall.

She had lunch with an old friend of Oliver, who promised he would help her in any way he could; and she was glad, and reasured because they had their affection for Oliver in common.

'How are you doing?' he asked.

Dreadful, she wanted to say, but she didn't want to break down. 'Just about all right,' she answered.

'I know it must be awful. You have to be strong.'

His hand snaked towards hers across the table. His eyes held mock concern. Snake. He was no different. His hand was now stroking hers — which she dared not withdraw because her good manners forbade it.

'I can look after you,' he said, encouraged. 'You need a man . . . You know, I've always found you incredibly attractive.'

Her senses prevailed. She stumbled to her feet — so abruptly that her glass fell and splintered on the floor, wine spilling everywhere, and her chair tumbled on its side. She stared. There was nothing she could say. She stared for a few seconds longer, then walked briskly past the approaching waiter and made her exit.

This degradation continued, doubly upsetting where she knew the wives. What did these men think she was? Who did they think *they* were?

She declined their invitations politely, because she didn't want to cause offence, but she felt repugnance with her whole being; her body that had been Oliver's; anything he wanted, anything they dared for him. And now it was solely hers. She was like an invalid. Life was a colossal boulder she couldn't negotiate.

'You must learn to,' Astrid said. Astrid, without whom she doubted she'd have survived.

'I can't. My soul's solid with dullness.'

'You can. I swear you can.'

The months of his illness, watching, waiting for him to die: nothing prepared her for the actuality.

'I never thought I wouldn't grow old with Oliver. Through all our troubles that thought never once occurred to me.'

Once he discussed death with her. He'd said, 'There's such a fine line in the transition between clinging on and that final glazing-over of the eyes . . . there's something. My instincts tell me there is, while all my scientific training makes a nonsense of it.'

And she could hear his voice, imbued with the fervent idealism of his house-doctor days – and Oliver, let there be something.

Gradually she learned; things most women had learned in their twenties. The sudden exposure was the hardest adjustment: she had always been sheltered. And she missed giving. Her abundance of love was redundant. Those old-fashioned urges in her which made her want to cosset a man, and lent domestic chores a purpose, lay fallow. She was fallow. And yet she had to pretend to be strong, to cope with her stroppy daughter.

• Valerie Blumenthal

She was tired of Windsor: the small-town suburban attitudes, the small talk, the wariness of wives now she was single. As a town it was neither one thing nor the other. It was a place for tourists. Christos, who had accepted his fate as though he had indeed written it, had long ago been whisked away by his powerful mother. Harriet thought of him often and her dreams of Oliver would sometimes incorporate him. She had no real friends here. The house offered her nothing, and it was rambling. The clothes horse in the bath was bare and ugly without Oliver's shirts and underwear on it.

Spring. April. Five months one week and two days since Oliver died; and she returned home from teaching to find the house had been burgled. She couldn't believe it. Every drawer pulled out and upturned. The contents of every cupboard spilled onto the floor in an act of spiteful callousness and no point. She stood in the doorway to her bedroom surveying the devastation, and *she* was devastated, could not bear this final brutal blow. Their lives, their organised, intimate lives strewn all over the place. Her fragile strength crumbled and she sank down in the crater of the wreckage, feeling as though she had just been widowed again.

The police arrived. 'What seems to be missing?' the young one asked, notepad in hand. 'Is anything of value gone?'

And ridiculously she hadn't considered what was missing, only the mess.

'Is my owl gone?' screeched Natasha when she returned from her cello lesson – and bounded upstairs. 'He's here,' she called down, as if nothing else on earth mattered. 'He's still here.'

And Harriet had a desire to laugh and laugh. 'Halleluja,' she called back sarcastically.

And so began the arduous task of tidying up, and as she did so, as she put away their lives again and touched familiar things, it seemed to her that the house had been blotted with sin.

What's missing? Is there anything of value gone?

Yes. My husband. My partner.

The carriage clock was missing, the silver-plate cutlery and candlesticks were missing, her jewellery – not that she had owned much – was missing; antique ornaments, Oliver's pewter collection, her father's Hunter watch, the portable television, Natasha's camera, one of her own paintings. In different circumstances she could have been flattered. More was missing than not.

She told Astrid, 'I look at everyone I once trusted – the dustmen, the gardener, the postman, and think was it you, or you. That's the worst of it. Not trusting anyone anymore. The house will never be the same again.'

'So move,' Astrid said.

'Move,' Harriet reiterated, shocked. 'How could I move?'

'Easily.'

'Where to?'

'London of course. Near me.'

That night in the bedroom that no longer seemed like hers, her mind was churning.

I'd live in a hovel with you.

How about one in Parson's Green?

And a twinge, the barest stirring of optimism, that night of the burglary, five months one week and two days after her widowhood.

• • •

Gnat and Robert have fallen out; she feels so down about it, had come to regard him as 'hers'. She hasn't a clue what she's done wrong – there's not been a quarrel, nothing like that – but he's avoiding her. So now she's resorted to being narky in return, even though inside her she doesn't feel like it. Into an envelope with 'Up Yours' scrawled on it, go the four jumping beans, and she thrusts it at him while he's watching *Neighbours*. She'll show him he's not the be all and end all, snipes at him about his old-fashioned clothes or his hopelessness at maths in class. It's become a game, which would be fun if she didn't care so much; he'll walk past her, head down and she'll pull a face at him and snipe at him with a jibe. Sometimes he glances at her from the other side of the room with an expression she can't fathom, then looks quickly away again. She doesn't understand what's changed and gloomily mulls over the unfairness of it all, how just when you're starting to be vaguely happy about something it all goes wrong and you become unhappy again.

Fuck him, she says to herself several times. Once to him. Fuck you. But doesn't mean it.

Maria's making her some earrings and that cheers her a little. Some blue stones she's set into tiny shells. And she's pierced new holes in Gnat's ears with a properly sterilised hot needle and cork.

'Does it hurt?'

'No. Not really. Not much worse than the gun-way.'

'It's much slower though. Tell me if it hurts.'

Maria really cares about her.

Gone midnight and the pair of them crouch before the ouija board in the bathroom, the letters arranged on the lavatory lid. Gnat's owl presides. Shadows flicker and leap on the wall, and in the candlelight the girls' faces are ivory and grey. Gnat can scarcely breathe. Her heart is as though an albatross is trapped there, beating its wings.

'Is anyone there? Speak to us, spirits. Please speak to us and tell us if anyone's there.'

Maria's voice is eerie and hoarse. Their index fingers rest, quivering, on the glass. Nothing happens and Gnat is both relieved and disappointed.

'You really need more than two people,' Maria explains.

'Can I try asking?' Gnat says.

'Sure.'

Gnat repeats Maria's invocation in a tremulous tone, and after a few seconds feels something happening: a magnetic pull on her finger as the glass very slowly creeps from its central position. Her heart is almost bursting; the candle flames dancing. Her eyes are riveted to the glass as it starts to move freely – their fingers scarcely touching it – to the letters.

The first is an M, so that they assume the message will be for Maria. But the glass moves swiftly to an I, then, twice, to S.

'Miss?' whispers Maria, taken aback.

But Gnat knows. Her mouth becomes dry and she waits in terrified suspense as the glass spells out her surname. Only her father called her that.

May I come in, Miss Edwards?

You may, Doctor Edwards.

She is shivering, her teeth chattering whilst the glass speeds from letter to letter and repeatedly spells three words: cello. Mum. Happ. No Y at the end. Maria talks to the 'spirits,' interrogates them and Gnat, too frozen to participate, feels her finger tugged in all directions, as the glass whizzes indiscriminately. But other than those three words the letters make no sense. There is definitely something in the room: a presence. If it's her father's, why is she so frightened, unable to breathe? The atmosphere is evil. Whatever force is there is overpowering her.

Maria suddenly sits bolt upright, her features contort and her voice deepens, and in horror Gnat witnesses her metamorphosis into her alter ego, the high priestess: imperious and malevolent. Gnat screams, leaping up so that the glass shatters on the floor and the letters scatter. Grabbing her owl, she escapes from the bathroom, from the spirits, and Maria who is not Maria; the albatross flapping its wings in her chest as she runs back to the dormitory.

'Have you considered how hard it must have been for your mother to be continually rejected by you?' Dr Middleton says.

'But she didn't need me. She always had other people fussing over her. Daddy, then Elliot. Everyone I cared about she took over. Gabble, gabble. She and Astrid gabble for hours. Even Dimple. Dimple spent ages talking with her instead of me.'

'But your mother didn't have *you*, her daughter. And her husband died. It's a dreadful thing to lose one's partner.'

'She met Elliot quickly enough. And there were others before him.'

'Other boyfriends?'

'I don't know if they were boyfriends properly.'

She likes the way his eyes burrow into hers and wishes he'd get rid of the soppy photographs of his wife and son on the desk. She wonders what it would be like to be French-kissed by him.

'Gnat?'

Little does he know her thoughts – not those, anyway!

'She shouldn't have wanted to be with other men. I mean it wasn't fair on Daddy. How could she have loved Daddy?'

'It was partly because she loved your father that she needed to have a loving relationship again.'

Lately her mother's image has a habit of springing unbidden to her mind, and she appears now, drooping-shouldered and defeated. Gnat tries to banish her.

'Look what's the point of all this? She hates me anyway, so I'll never be going back.'

'Did these men stay the night?' he presses her, without, apparently, having heard what she said.

'Only Elliot. But they make this great thing about pretending he sleeps in the spare room. I know he sneaks into hers later. They must think I'm a sucker.'

'Doesn't your mother have a right to her own happiness, Gnat? To a life of her own? She might seem old to you, but she's actually a young and attractive woman.'

His words jab a raw spot in her. How many times has she wished her mother were plain? Not so plain as to be ashamed of her, but enough to attract less attention. More boring-looking. Elliot is three years younger than her; an architect. Tall and sensitive-faced, he resembles Jeremy Irons. Sometimes play-acting in front of the mirror, Gnat pretended her mother had gone to live abroad and Elliot was her guardian and fell in love with her.

She liked to see him in the mornings: rumpled-featured, padding about with a towel round his waist. He was like a thin bear with his hair sticking up all over the place. In the second bathroom, which she used, the sight of his brush, razor and sponge bag amongst her shampoos and bubblebaths made her happy. She would chatter to him from the doorway while he shaved, fascinated by the way he pulled his cheeks about like a piece of elastic; and the razor made sandpaper sounds against his skin as he scraped away at his stubble and the white foam, leaving paths of beige. She would be reminded of her father then, and her nose would smart with wanting to cry.

But now she's a bit in love with Dr Middleton, who toys with her life, who stirs her emotions as though they're the ingredients of a Christmas cake and knows almost everything there is to about her. She's also a bit in love with Robert still, and slightly with a boy from her past called Phillip, the son of one of her mother's friends, and of whom, for some reason, she keeps dreaming. In her dreams he's doing 'things' to her.

Remembering: one particular night when Elliot stayed. She'd drunk some cooking wine when her mother wasn't looking, and then polished off the contents of Elliot's glass. Tipsy, she went to her bedroom where she smoked a cigarette. Her head was echoing and she stubbed out the stale cigarette, undressed, put on her tee-shirt with the skull printed on it, and climbed into bed. She wished she had blond hair and golden skin; and bones that showed. She'd go blond one day. In the magazine *Just Seventeen* it said blondes were out; and studs. Just when she'd plucked up the guts to have hers done. Anyway, what was wrong with studs? Asian women had worn them for centuries, and her mother always cooed over the way they got themselves up.

She felt dizzy, drifted towards sleep, then heard them coming upstairs; their whispering before they parted. Wide awake now, she decided what to do. She waited for about twenty minutes then crept from her room. The crack under her mother's door was dark, and she went from there to the spare room.

'Harriet,' Elliot whispered.

For an instant Gnat was taken aback. 'It's me,' she hissed, and slid into his bed.

'Gnat! What on earth are you doing here?'

She snuggled close to him and he lay there rigidly. 'I want to be with you.'

It was all she wanted: to fall asleep by him. He was warm, his skin sweet smelling.

'For God's sake Gnat, get out.' He sat up, his hand pushing on her back.

Her head span. She was like a chicken on a spit. Her legs and body were leaden. 'Can I go to sleep with you Elliot? Elliot, ple-e-ease.'

He put his arm round her and kissed her hair.

'Can I marry you?' she asked.

He laughed softly. 'I think I'm too old for you. Now listen, you must return to your own bed, darling.'

She loved him calling her that. 'I want to sleep here. Let me sleep here.'

'No.'

'Why?'

'You know exactly why.'

She did not. She wanted only to draw comfort from his nearness.

But he got up and hauled her to her feet. He kissed her fondly on either cheek, and she went dejectedly to her room. Later, when her eyelids were growing heavy, and colours and shapes formed dancing sprites in her head, she heard him going to her mother. Tears slid down her nose and she blotted them with her owl.

The episode seems very distant. Everything unconnected to Turner's End seems distant.

'Do you think perhaps it was a spiteful thing to do, to climb into bed with your mother's boyfriend?' Dr Middleton asks.

'I didn't do it to be spiteful. I mean I just did it. When I got to his room I knew that I didn't want to do anything – you know, anything – with him. I only wanted to be near him to sleep.'

'Gnat, we can't always do just what we like. We have to consider other people.'

She glares down at the floor.

'Do you want people to be angry with you, to dislike you?'

'I don't know.'

'Come on Gnat, of course you know.'

'I guess not, then.' Her foot plays with the edge of the rug.

'And would you want some of the things that you do and say, done and said to you?'

'But I only say things when I'm got at or when I'm down. Everyone always gets at me. I mean I'm just me. I don't think about things I'm saying or doing. They just happen.' And look where she's ended up as a result.

'And other people are just *themselves* and they have feelings too. You must try and see their points of view besides your own. You must learn to think before you act. Do you understand what I'm saying?'

'I suppose.'

'You do, I know, because you're an intelligent girl. Extremely intelligent, in fact. And talented. You could do all kinds of things if you wanted. Now, you mentioned that you say things because you're down, are you down a lot of the time?'

'I guess so.'

'Why, Gnat?'

'I don't know. I miss Daddy. I have a thing inside me. It's like a stone.'

'Sometimes being nice to people can get rid of that stone. Sometimes being horrid can actually cause it.'

Her vision becomes blurry. She wants to lie down and howl for hours and hours.

'Self-esteem, Gnat,' he reminds her.

She doesn't answer; upset about Robert, tired from last night with the ouija board, upset about Maria, upset about the message: Cello. Mum. Happ. Mum. Harriet . . . Hurting because of her.

'I didn't mean to hurt her,' she murmurs brokenly.

In the recreation room she avoids Maria.

'Why aren't you talking to me?' the girl asks, cornering her later, and Gnat blurts out the truth.

'I can't help it,' Maria says. 'I'm blacked out, aren't I? I don't know what I'm doing. I remember doing the board, then blackness.'

That night in the dormitory someone cries softly in the dark: Maria, whose parents don't want her, whom nobody knows what to do with; gloriously beautiful, gentle Maria who is a liability to herself and everyone around her. Gnat listens to her for a while before groping her way over to the other girl's bed. She curls up with her under the duvet with its pattern of harlequins, and Maria falls asleep, her breath coming in tiny wafts between parted lips. Gnat lies squashed beside her, mulling over her afternoon session with Dr Middleton.

I want to go home. I want to go home. I want to go home, chants the litany in her head.

8

'So we moved,' Harriet reminisces. 'In the summer, eight months after my husband's death. Another doctor bought the house, well a surgeon actually.'

The wife, an interior designer, given to loud exclamations punctuated with the clapping of hands, referred to Harriet's flamboyant use of colour as quaint, and said wouldn't it be boring if everyone's taste was the same? Very, she agreed dismally, listening to the woman prattling about curtains with swags, and the English country-house look.

'Fucking bitch,' drawled Astrid, there when the woman was calling out window measurements to her assistant.

'They've overpaid for the house,' Harriet said. 'It makes it easier to bite your tongue.'

'She was bloody rude about Hilda.'

Hilda was the large stone hippopotamus which served as a doorstop in the breakfast room.

'Hilda's thick-skinned.' She joked with a wan smile of bravado.

From another room rang out the surgeon's wife's strident tones: 'Five foot three, times three foot nine . . . Goodness, how *anyone* could have –' And then her voice was lost.

Now that the move was imminent she was beset with doubts. The house seemed to embrace her afresh and to reproach her. Natasha threw tantrums, called her mother a traitor and cut up photographs of Harriet and Oliver, leaving only him. Harriet, too weary and depressed to argue, ignored her. She was afraid to tackle her. It was easier to shut her ears to the abuse.

'If only I'd been braver,' she says. 'There was just too much going on, with the move and everything.'

The psychiatrist smiles wisely and she pulls a rueful expression.

'I rather suspect you've heard that before. If only.'

'I don't know anybody who wouldn't have benefited from hindsight at some time or another,' he tells her. 'I always say that hindsight is sent to mock us.'

It was school holidays; they packed up their old life. Chaos reigned. Harriet attempted to be organised: made a note to sweep the mouse poison from behind the fridge and remove the trap from under the sink (Murderess, accused Natasha, who had her own pet white mouse called Rodent, and had become vegetarian); remembered to pay the newspaper and milk bills to date; to inform the post office, the DVLC office, the insurance company and God knows who else, of her change of address. So much to think of. How did other women manage on their own? And what about nights, when their bodies drove them mad with sexual urges which had no entitlement?

The boxes piled up and took over the house, and Harriet recalled when she and Oliver had first moved to Windsor and they hardly possessed anything apart from basic furniture, books and cassettes. Pale patches and holes were left on walls where pictures were removed, and carpet stains which had been concealed by stragetically placed chairs, were revealed. The house, like a tired woman, looked as though it had fallen into disrepair. Not that it mattered: the new people were intending to gut it, to transform it into a home befitting a surgeon with a private practice instead of a NHS general practitioner.

She unhooked the curtains, and the avenue was exposed from the sitting room window – and scratching around the chestnut tree on the opposite side of the road was the pekinese who had indirectly caused Pirate's death. She lay on the carpet where she and Oliver had lain together; beseiged by memories. In her mind's eye she can still see herself lying there on that dirty old threadbare carpet, staring up at the plaster-moulding on the ceiling which became a frame for her memories.

'Natasha ran away the day of the move. Can you believe it? I had to give vacant possession by midday, the men were packed up, the new owners' lorry with their stuff was parked outside – and Natasha had disappeared. It was a nightmare. God, it was a nightmare.'

• • •

'I threw everything away because it was a part of my life that was over. I kept my puppets for doing plays though. My mother tipped everything out of the dustbin bags and made me put it all in order before putting it back. I even had to wrap up some things. It took hours. But there was nothing else to do anyway. I stopped going to the loft. I couldn't stand going in there anymore.'

'You say that that part of your life was over. Have you ever considered that perhaps your mother felt the same? That she wanted to make a fresh start?' Dr Middleton asks her.

'But she never asked me,' Gnat protests. 'She should've asked me what I wanted also.'

'Maybe she wanted to avoid a scene, or she assumed you would adjust. Maybe she thought she was doing what was best for you both and that you were too young to judge.'

'Best for her, you mean.'

'And what's so wrong with that?'

Gnat juts out her lower lip-in a scowl. But the lonely,

unresponsive atmosphere of the house comes back to her; it was like a nut kernel without the nut.

'She always thinks she's right about everything.'

The shelves in his room are crammed with books, and the title of one wrests her attention: *Behavioural disturbance in the adolescent*. Discomforted, she nonetheless finds herself drawn to it.

'Pretend you are a mother, Gnat,' Dr Middleton says.

And this makes her peal with spontaneous laughter; the idea is so outrageous.

But he continues seriously, 'You'd have to make decisions wouldn't you? And if your husband had just died, the burden of decision making would be extra hard. Think about it for a moment, please.'

She stops laughing. Briefly she is her mother, and she feels a gamut of emotions. She has a truculent daughter who shouts and argues, is rude, ungrateful, spiteful and secretive; who is clever and musically gifted; who deliberately sets out to make her mother miserable; who is full of festering anger and believes herself the saddest girl in the world. That girl whom Dr Middleton is steadily exorcising from the one seated opposite him.

'Not much fun, is it, being a mother on the receiving end?'

She shakes her head without replying.

'I cried my last day at school,' she confides after a long gap. 'I mean I wasn't mad about the school or anything, but I'd been there since I was five, and was leaving everything and everyone. I even cried saying goodbye to my cello teacher. I mean he wasn't that horrid after all. Dimple was so lucky. I was mad at her for being so lucky. I told her I wanted to run away then I wouldn't have to move, and she said her aunt who lived nearby was on holiday, and there was a summerhouse in the garden and I could hide there.'

*   *   *

They vowed eternal friendship, and in a solemn ritual pricked index fingers and squeezed out minute bubbles of blood which they rubbed together to make them blood sisters.

When Gnat returned home from school her mood of sorrow and anger was augmented by the sight of her mother knee-deep in newspaper, wrapping up crockery. She saw her as the cause of all her grievances, and, ignoring Harriet's gaunt and suffering face, she kicked at a ball of paper and went wordlessly to her bedroom, slamming the door behind her so that the wall vibrated.

The day of the move came; men arriving, tramping through the house with their thick shoes, calling to each other jovially as they packed yet more boxes and loaded the lorry – itself the size of a bungalow. 'We make moving a small m' was the slogan along the great slab of its side.

She hated their good humour. They were stacking away her happiness in that lorry, stripping the house like a chicken carcass, as if the Edwards had never lived there. One of them was carrying Hilda, tottering under her weight, and another, her cello – and Gnat could stand no more of it; with her owl grasped in her fist, her purse in her pocket, she escaped.

Her feet sped past familiar houses and buildings she'd known all her life; the church where she'd played her cello, the store belonging to the Indian grocer who gave her a small tub of satay sauce whenever she went in there. Zigzagging across roads, she came to where Dimple's aunt lived and, unseen, slipped into the summerhouse at the end of the garden. Inside were a pair of sun loungers and a single chair, folded and on its side; a lawnmower smelling of grass and oil; gardening tools; and a pair of earth-encrusted gloves stuffed into a watering can. Various packets, jars, pots and bottles cluttered the shelf. It all looked so homely.

She had nothing to do, nothing whatsoever to occupy

her except her thoughts. She unfolded the chair and sat in it, positioning it so she could see through the small panes of the glazed door: the neat lawn and box hedges, the container of bird feed dangling from the branch of a tree, and a half coconut with a bird balancing on it; the roofs of other houses; other gardens, and a cricket pitch beyond – kids playing on it, a couple of dogs chasing one another; the steeple of her church. And for a moment Gnat could hear choristers singing therein, and a young girl with a rapt expression giving a cello recital. And afterwards everyone coming up to her and patting her on the back, Well done, well done. The welling up of pride within her.

She play-acted. It hindered her not to have a mirror, but she could just make out her reflection in the glass panes, which would have to suffice. For half an hour she occupied herself in this way, then she became restless. She talked to her owl, composed a story for it, narrated extracts from *The Little Prince* – and recalled her mother sitting on the end of her bed crying over the ending with her. *Charlie and the Chocolate Factory* provided a diversion for a further half an hour, and then once more she was at a loss. And it was only just past midday. Midday, when they had to vacate their house. At this precise moment her mother would be frantically searching for her, calling her, doing her nut, perhaps even phoning the police.

She lasted almost four hours in there. At one stage she fell asleep and dreamed a lion was chasing her across scrubland. Finally, bursting to wee, her tummy rumbling from hunger, she emerged, took her knickers down and squatted behind the roses. Their scent filled her nostrils. Nothing to eat. Nothing to do. She decided to venture to the newsagents to buy some crisps and sweets. It was strange being on her own, nobody knowing of her whereabouts; a sensation that in fact she did not exist at all. She could observe and herself be unseen. And if she were invisible, who would notice her slipping a packet of crisps into her pocket? But she could not bring herself to steal. She bought several packets of chocolates and crisps, two comics, and left – automatically heading for home, before registering that it was not home anymore.

She had consumed her feast and read the comics. Night approached, and in the summerhouse, Gnat, afraid, gave a single sob. She heard it herself in the alien silence, like a hiccough. A car drew up and a door slammed; then another. But she took no notice until looking through the glass door she was able to discern two approaching figures of differing heights behind the tunnelled beam of a torch: Dimple and her father. She was both relieved and infuriated.

'I had to tell them,' Dimple cried out defensively, before Gnat could say anything. 'They've all been going crazy. You're mother's been phoning. I pretended I didn't know anything, but in the end they made me tell them. They made me. They got hold of the police. It wasn't my fault. Don't look at me like that.'

• • •

Summer is finished. Day after day of drizzle and greyness rob the sky of its luscious sun. The weather fills Harriet with despair. It is symbolic of the general mess surrounding her. She can see no solution to the problem with her daughter. And the kindly man opposite her, doesn't he grow bored of listening to her rambling? and not only her, but numerous others, all wallowing in their hang-ups. Does his brain never object, 'Enough. I've heard enough from you all to last me a lifetime; rubbish to the lot of you'?

She giggles out loud.

'What is it?' he enquires.

When she tells him he gives a small chuckle. 'I enjoy

riddles,' he says. 'And the mind is the most interesting riddle of all.'

Their new home was a white cottage in a square punctuated with chestnut and cherry trees: conkers in autumn, blossom in spring. And at the back of the cottage was a long garden and a swing suspended from the apple tree, where Harriet would sit for long periods swinging slowly back and forth with the pendulum of her thoughts.

Those early weeks, when the house was strange to her, and she to it, she was conscious of every noise and would leap up to investigate: the pipes, the creaks of walls, squeaks of doors. She discovered the location of switches and sockets, and that the hot water from her bath tap trickled then gushed, that the central heating system worked back to front, and not at all with the towel-rail on.

She painted walls in primary colours that would have made the surgeon's wife grimace, embellishing them with murals and stencilled borders. She altered curtains and hung pictures. Hilda ruled the sitting room with an Indian tasselled mat on her broad back, a moving-in present from Astrid.

'A triumph,' was Astrid's verdict of the house.

Natasha mooched about, watching her mother's display of energy morosely.

'Why don't you ring Dimple?' Harriet suggested. But her daughter had not yet forgiven her friend for her betrayal.

'I hate this crummy place. I hate this house.'

'You could go riding in Hyde Park.'

'Who wants to go riding in draggy Hyde Park? Boring, boring, boring.'

'I could take you to Windsor then. It's not far.'

'Leave me alone. Stop nagging me.'

And Hariet resisted the desire to grab her daughter, to shake and shake her.

A house where Oliver had never been. His photographs were in every room, his comb on Harriet's dressing table, watch on her wrist, few clothes in her wardrobe. Her bedroom was her private haven, whose sloping ceilings she had transformed into a Bedouin tent; and her studio, in reality a large original conservatory, was perfect. She filled it with plants and installed her easel in there and her artist's paraphanalia; and from time to time was happy – before rebuking herself for allowing it.

'After the first few weeks I knew I'd done the right thing, moving. People weren't suspicious of me. There was none of that suburban gossip behind shielding hands. I made new friends. There was always something to see or do.'

Memories would not hinder her progress.

'And it was right for Natasha. She was growing up. There was more to occupy her. I went away for a week. Natasha patched up her quarrel with Dimple and stayed with her. And I went away. It was a ridiculously big decision to make, that step of going away for the first time on my own.'

It was the end of August, and at the old inn where she stayed in a village on the edge of Dartmoor, Harriet knew she was the subject of speculation and hid behind books when she sat by herself. A London businessman, there for the fishing, ruddy, confident-faced and prosperous-bellied, mistook her politeness for interest. He insisted she join him at his table in the evenings, though she would have preferred to have remained alone with her book, without the effort of enforced conversation. He plied her with drink and questioned her about her divorce. When he learned she was a widow, he veered from the topic as though she'd announced she was a heroin addict.

She was discovering that people did not know how to deal with her widowed state, that men were threatened by it and did not know how to compete against somebody who, though dead, was a stronger force than themselves.

• Valerie Blumenthal

In their desire to exorcise a ghost they were afraid to let her talk about her marriage. She wasn't allowed to have a past; as far as they were concerned Oliver had never existed; but they spoke uninhibitedly about their relationships, their divorces. Elliot was the first man secure enough, generous enough, to encourage her to talk.

The businessman's room was next to hers. She heard him gargling and belching and coughing; the lavatory flushing, bath running, clothes hangers being pushed about in his wardrobe. She moved about like a mouse so that he would have no part of her privacy.

In the mornings she woke early and after breakfast went for long walks. Her arms and legs were bare and brown, her breasts bra-less in a tee-shirt. She walked with her effortless stride until she came to her favourite spot, where a waterfall hurtled between rocks and the foam sparkled like shards of glass as it trapped the sun. The escarpment of hills in the background was matt copper with bracken. And she would lie on the bank, arms tucked beneath her head to cushion it from tree roots, watching tiny creatures busying themselves amidst leaves and moss, scurrying about with purpose, the rushing of water a constant, soothing throb, feeling her mind empty and something akin to well-being nourishing her.

'You shouldn't look that good,' the businessman told her at dinner on her last night. He'd ordered Champagne and he topped up her glass. 'It's not fair on a bloke's blood pressure.'

Harriet, slightly drunk, failed to think of a witty response and grinned inanely. Later, when he asked her to go to bed with him, she demurred then consented. Nine months since Oliver's death, and her neglected body clamoured for attention. In her inebriated condition it seemed to her that the man was attractive after all. She trailed behind him to his room; it was larger than hers and untidy. A mobile phone lay amongst papers and a bunch of keys and money on the table. Without preliminaries, he pulled her to him.

I've changed my mind, her sane self cried out, while her polite self, her drunk self, complied as he pushed her, a half naked trophy of no worth, onto the bed.

He turned her roughly on her stomach, ramming into her from behind, his unshaven cheek grazing hers. And she tensed against him, pinioned there, half suffocated by pillows, wishing it was over; degraded and ashamed, loathing him and herself.

'Do you always just lie there?' he said afterwards, putting on his striped towelling robe as she hauled on her skirt and fumbled with the hook.

Humiliated, utterly sober, and sore, she said what she'd longed to say to every man who'd attempted to get her into bed.

'You bastard.'

In her own bathroom she ran the water. She was shivering. She felt contaminated. And she had betrayed Oliver. Through the thin walls she heard the man snoring, and she was disgusted at the thought of him inside her. *She* was disgusting.

'Bastard,' she repeated to herself. 'Bastard;' inserting the soap deep inside her, to rid herself of all traces of him.

In bed she ached anew for Oliver, for tender fingers rippling over her skin, for his belly with its soft hairs upon hers, for his caring doctor's ringed eyes. And the rest of her life without him.

How easy it would be with a bottle of Panadol. But there again, there were moments – as when she dozed on the riverbank with the filtered sun on her upturned face, or painted amongst the pungent-smelling jungle in her conservatory – moments which prevented her doing anything about her vague contemplations.

At breakfast the next morning she and the man studiously

ignored each other. Did the other guests notice? Were they talking about her, that 'fast' woman on her own? She paid her bill and left; drove back to London – turning off the M4 at the Windsor junction before remembering that she no longer lived there.

9

'H-h-hi Gn-gn-gnat,' Robert said as he passed her on the stairs, suddenly lifting his head and looking at her in the old way.

So they're friends again. She has no idea what has prompted this mood reversal – who knows anything in this place – but is forgiving; she's just so glad. But her gladness is nevertheless tempered with suspicion and this time she's keeping a bit of herself apart. Perhaps she rushed things before. This time she'll play it cooler and see what happens. And she's learned you can't trust anybody, even people you think you can.

Friday afternoon, and the prospect of another weekend looming at Turner's End. Robert goes home. His mother fetches him. She looks like him. He waves cheerfully as he leaves and calls out to Gnat, 'See you Sunday evening,' singling her out. She waves back with a deliberate take-it-or-leave-it nonchalance; friendly, but not too friendly. Some others go home also. Not Gnat. Not Maria, or Jason or Lisa ... The rejects. One big happy family; and this weekend The Spoon is planning to take them to Chessington Zoo.

'Who's going to look at who?' quips Gnat, dressed in a short black skirt, black waistcoat, black tights and Doc Martens. Most of her clothes are black, embellished with safety pins and chains and badges. Lately she has found herself wishing she had some different clothes.

'We're a bunch of monkeys,' she adds. 'Shove us behind bars and see the spectacle. Throw nuts at us. Monkey nuts. Nuts – get it? I hate zoos. They're cruel. I'm not coming, thanks.'

'That's a shame. We'll miss you.'

'But don't you see? The more people who visit zoos, the more animals will go on being held in captivity.'

'I was hoping I could have you as my second-in-command,' The Spoon wheedles.

Gnat shakes her head decisively. 'I can't, I'm sorry. But I just won't go to zoos or circuses.'

'Well then, I must respect your views.'

She glances at the nurse suspiciously for some sign that she is being mocking, but there is nothing spurious in The Spoon's placid gaze and Gnat saunters off to Dr Middleton's room whistling, congratulating herself that she has abided by her principles without getting worked-up. Being rational, Dr Middleton would call it.

He isn't there and she makes herself comfortable in her usual chair, a piece of music by Haydn that she was playing earlier on her cello running through her head. Absently she fiddles with the dog-and-ball charm on her silver bracelet she has taken to wearing.

The psychiatrist bursts in. 'Sorry I'm late, sorry I'm late,' he apologises, reminding her of the white rabbit in *Alice in Wonderland*, running his fingers through his hair. 'My wife's just had a baby girl.' His face is a giant grin stretching from ear to ear.

'That's great,' she says, surprised to find she means it.

He stretches and retracts his neck several times like a tortoise, crosses his legs – his trousers always ride up above his socks, showing a pale expanse of calf with straggling black hairs on it – and laces his hands. This is always her cue; and she plucks from her mind, thinking how funny it is there is always something to extract, like a lucky-dip.

'My mother and I never discussed Daddy. I mean we didn't discuss anything much, but I never knew what she was feeling, about Daddy. I guess she must have missed him ... The girls at my new school were all nice to me to begin with because they were sorry for me. They were really wet. You know – sniggering behind their hands over pathetic things, copying each other's work, having crushes on the teachers. And catty as hell. You know, ganging up and all that. And we had this poncy uniform. Everyone was such a snob, and sneaky. Telling tales and sucking up.'

Her first day; and her mother deposited her in the headmistress's stifling little room and left her in a line-up of twenty other new girls – a sickly-smiling, apprehensive group except for one with sly black eyes called Felicity. The pair assessed each other and tacitly acknowledged instant enmity. And then, in the midst of the headmistress extolling the school to them, Gnat became conscious of a vile smell pervading the room. She started giggling. Somebody had trodden in dog shit.

'What's the matter Natasha?' asked Miss Pugh.

'Nothing.'

'I expect you're just nervous, are you dearie?'

'Not really.'

And then came the dreadful discovery. As she lifted her foot slightly she noticed dark stains on the carpet. It was herself. She had trodden in it. Scarlet-faced, she stood there shifting her feet, sniffing the air and looking accusingly at the other pupils as though they were the culprits. They started staring round also, and soon everyone was sniffing and blushing. She noticed Miss Pugh surreptitiously raise her foot to inspect underneath, and suddenly the room felt unbearably hot and Gnat's cheeks were on fire. Beside her, Felicity gave a snort of laughter.

'It's rather hot isn't it girls?' the headmistress said. 'Better have some fresh air. We don't want you all suffocating on your first day, do we now?'

'No, Miss Pugh,' came the chorus in reply.

Silly old bat, Gnat thought. She looks like a pug. Pug-faced Pugh.

She scraped her foot furtively along the carpet all the way to her classroom. It transpired Felicity was in the same one and knew most of the other girls, and they surrounded her, ignoring Gnat, until one pupil with a long plait and intense eyes approached her, and offered her a peppermint.

'I don't like peppermints.'

'Oh.' The girl was unsettled by Gnat's outspokenness. 'What does your father do?'

'He's dead.'

'Oh. Oh you poor thing. You can sit next to me if you like. We can choose at the beginning of term.'

She went off to inform the others and within seconds they had deserted Felicity to crowd round Gnat and ply her with sweets.

But the novelty of her having no father wore thin and her popularity did not endure; she made no attempt to mix with the others, to partake in discussions as to whose father was richest, or mother the most beautiful; whose brother went to the most parties; who had been French-kissed. And soon, headed by Felicity, they formed a gang against her.

They took revenge on her for rebuffing their generosity by ostracising her completely. They spilt ink over her homework, whispered obviously about her and wrote her malicious, anonymous notes. I don't care, Gnat convinced herself. She shortened her skirt two inches above her plump knees and chewed gum which she stuck under different desks or on the insides of lids. To the bewilderment of the teachers, she came top in almost every subject while appearing not to concentrate in lessons, sang like a bird, and passed her grade six cello exam with distinction. The pupils disliked her more than ever.

At first Gnat's misdemeanours were minor: talking in class, her short skirt, rudeness, bringing her walkman to school, chewing gum, caught trying to free the half-bald parrot from a cage smaller than her mouse's; walking out of the scripture lesson because God was a berk. All these things were excusable because of her circumstances. They did not know that at break she slipped off to the local boys' school and exchanged kisses and a quick feel of her breasts (through her jumper) for cigarettes. She hid them in a packet of cigarette-sweets where they were almost indistinguishable.

'Do you enjoy smoking, Gnat?' Dr Middleton asks.

'Not particularly.'

'So why do you do it?'

'Well I suppose it's cool. I mean all the kids do it. You're left out if you don't.'

'Is it cool that smoking gives you the disease which killed your father?'

'You don't think of that though, not when you're doing it.'

'But you should.'

Pensively she rests her chin in the cupped palms of her hands. 'Well anyway, I don't feel like smoking now.'

'Why?'

'Well, everything's different, isn't it?'

'In what way?'

'Well I'm here for a start.'

'Uh-huh.' He waits expectantly.

Grudgingly, she obliges. 'I suppose I feel different. I mean a lot of what I did before was for show. I'm not like that so much now.'

'And which way are you more content with yourself?'

She examines her black-clad legs, pulls and releases the thick fabric of her tights. 'As I am now, I guess.' Making the hole on her thigh bigger with her finger.

When he asks her nothing further she continues, 'So anyway, Mummy was reading this—'

'Repeat that.'

'What you just said.'

'I was about to say my mother was reading a letter Pug-face sent her. What's wrong with that?'

'No matter,' he answers, something in his expression discomforting her. 'Go on.'

Harriet read the letter to her while Gnat assumed a total lack of interest. The second paragraph began,

> 'I regret to have to tell you that your daughter has a disruptive influence on the other girls, and whilst the staff have repeatedly made allowances for her behaviour I am sure you will appreciate there has to be a limit. I sincerely hope that Natasha will prevail upon herself to alter her attitude so that she might remain at Foskett House and benefit from all it has to offer ...'

'I mean they wanted their fat fees didn't they? Enough to feed a hundred Ethiopian families for two years or more.'

'How did your mother respond to the letter?'

'She didn't yell or anything. She sounded – she just sounded kind of tired. She just read the letter then went out of my room without really saying anything. I wished she'd yelled.'

'Why?'

'I don't know.'

'Could it be so you could then yell back and the blame would be shifted?'

'I've told you, I don't know. I mean you feel something

and then it's gone. You don't stop to analyse it at the time do you?'

Her mother making a stiff, silently reproachful exit from the room and Gnat longing for some reaction. The gentle, recriminating click of the door, leaving Gnat oddly deflated.

'I thought she no longer cared what I did.'

'And that mattered to you, even though you continually tested her?'

'I think so. I mean I just didn't know how to go about things anymore. So I became angrier inside me.'

'Uh-huh.'

'Well, in the end, after six months I was expelled. I put the school up for sale. I phoned an estate agent and he turned up and nobody could understand what he was doing there.'

She gives a hoot of laughter at the memory. 'I bragged about it to a girl I thought was my friend and she split. I didn't mind. For good measure I smeared superglue on Pug-face's telephone when she was gone from the room. Her ear got stuck. They had to cut the wire. Oh God, it was funny.' She bursts out laughing again, doubled up, clutching her knees.

'It was an iniquitous thing to do,' the psychiatrist tells her, his face creased in laughter also.

'What does that mean?'

'Wicked. Evil.'

Immediately she is serious, and wipes her streaming eyes with the back of her hands. 'I'm not evil, am I?'

'No, Gnat. You're not.'

He loans her a book as she leaves. 'I think you'll enjoy it.'

She looks at it: *The Prophet* by Kahlil Gibran; a slender paperback with an illustration of a man's gaunt face on the cover.

'I don't think it's my kind of book,' she says awkwardly.

'Take it anyway,' he urges. 'There's no hurry.'

Back in her dormitory she finds Susan punching the curtains in the belief someone is hiding behind them, because they are billowing in the breeze from the open window.

Gnat goes over to her chest of drawers. She has found her stud at last – it had fallen into a drawer – and is about to re-site it in her nostril when she stops. She examines her small pointed face in the mirror, a pixie-face with dark-lashed navy eyes. Her father's eyes, she realises with sudden pleasure. Her cheeks are still pink from laughter. She can't remember the last time she laughed so much. It must have been years ago. And in a few days she will be fourteen.

'Susan, if you stop punching the curtains I'll give you a present.'

'What?' the other girl asks mistrustfully, caught in motion, arm poised.

'Come and see.'

Susan ambles over to her with her odd crab-like gait and Gnat opens her hand to show her the stud.

'It's been in your nose,' Susan protests.

'Not for ages it hasn't. I can wash it.'

In the bathroom Susan holds the stud under the running tap. It slips from her fingers and is washed down the plug hole.

Gnat watches in dismay. 'Stupid. You're stupid. What did you do that for?' she cries.

'I didn't do it on purpose did I?'

'How would I know, in this stupid place?'

'My dad raped me when I was twelve.' Maria whispers to her that night.

'I don't believe you.'

'I swear it's true.'

On Maria's forearm is a tattoo: a heart with the words, 'I love my dad,' inside it.

'That's disgusting,' Gnat says, shocked.

And Maria starts crying. 'No it's not, no it's not. And it wasn't my dad. I wish it had been. It was a teacher at school. I wanted it to be my dad.'

'But how could you? I mean – your dad's your *dad*.'

'You can talk. You're a fine one to talk.'

The following day while everyone is at the zoo, Gnat lies on her bed reading the book Dr Middleton has lent her, and discovers it to be a cross between a work of philosophy and poetry, the counsel of a prophet to his fellow citizens before he embarks on the ship which will transport him back to the isle of his birth. In turn, they pose him questions; and Gnat is captivated by the wisdom and beauty of his advice.

Of love he wrote:

'But if in your fear you would seek only Love's peace and Love's pleasure
Then it is better for you that you cover your nakedness and Pass out of Love's threshing floor
Into the seasonless world where you shall laugh, but not all
Your laughter, and weep, but not all of your tears ...'

Gnat comes to a passage where the prophet is asked about Good and Evil, and she reads it with particular interest:

'Of the Good in you I can speak, but not of the Evil.
For what is Evil but good tortured by its own hunger and thirst?
Verily when Good is hungry it seeks food even in dark caves,
And when it thirsts it drinks even of dead waters.
You are Good when you are one with yourself.
Yet when you are not one with yourself you are not evil ...'

On and on she reads. The others return noisily and she ignores them, has galloped, excited and completely absorbed, through the entire book and gone back to the beginning, unable to put it aside, wanting to dwell again on its beauty, wanting to commit all she can to memory. Through the night, by torchlight, she reads it a third time; and when finally her head pounds and eyes will not remain open she falls asleep, filled with a sense of serenity, one sentence imprinted forever in her mind: 'When you are not one with yourself you are not evil.'

• • •

The Italian café owner who looks like Christos, brings Harriet a cappucino. This is her regular haunt and one of the walls is hung with her paintings which he sells on a commission basis – an arrangement which works well except when he becomes too amorous. This morning she has indicated she wants to be left alone and he sulks pointedly while Harriet sits at the small round marble-topped table sucking the end of her pen and pondering on what to write in her daughter's birthday cards.

The front of the main one is illustrated with a dog chasing its own tail, and, inside, the wording, 'Happy birthday from somebody you can reach.'

She had deliberated in the shop before buying it, gone from card to card before returning to this one. And now, pen poised, what else is there to add to its printed message? Have a lovely day? Natasha, stuck at Turner's End for her fourteenth birthday. Have a lovely day. And Harriet, who hasn't seen her since that disastrous afternoon, is racked with guilt.

'Here's to a good year,' she writes in the end, underlining 'good.' She signs it, 'Lots of love Mummy,' and adds a hypocritical kiss; stares grimly at her own handwriting, the short, meaningless message and puts the card in an envelope. She then writes in the other one she has bought, on behalf of the mouse – Rodent Mark 2 – and the spaniel.

Fourteen, she thinks, and such torment and confusion compacted into that young body. And sitting here with her coffee and birthday cards and the smoke of cigarettes from other tables drifting towards her, Harriet realises with a jolt of sorrow that she will look back on her daughter's childhood and adolescence with no pleasure whatsoever.

Remembering: sitting in Miss Pugh's boiling hot study while the headmistress catalogued her daughter's crimes; Natasha, stony-faced and unrepentant beside her. But the thing which saddened her most was when, after a term at the comprehensive school, Natasha announced in her newly acquired cockney accent that she was giving up the cello. There was nothing Harriet could do. Her daughter – her decisions, her life – was beyond her control. Natasha knew all her mother's weaknesses and vulnerable spots.

Harriet gave her a dress allowance and Natasha spent it on strange jewellery and clothes from second hand shops which she cut up and re-made into extraordinary creations, disappearing into her room for hours as she had as a small child. Occasionally she brought home friends – youngsters with shaven heads or bright crests – but usually, thankfully, she went to their homes. At weekends they went 'clubbing.' Not yet thirteen, and bopping at discos. And up to God knows what else.

Very occasionally, when Harriet did exercise her maternal authority, Natasha would release a torrent of invective so abusive that her mother would be reeling from it. But, she realises now with new and enlightening insight, Natasha always obeyed her.

Incidents flash before her: Rodent Mark 2 escaping from its cage and landing in the spaniel's playful jaws. Natasha nearly hysterical, and Harriet trying to keep calm, prising the puppy's jaws apart and rescuing the terrified but unscathed mouse; cooking vegetarian rissoles, and ironing the extraordinary clothes; tidying the chaotic room from time to time. And then she would be gripped by a spasm of fierce love as she surveyed the emblems of childhood – soft toys, old ornaments, her owl – juxtaposed with the symbols of womanhood: tights and tampons, makeup and jewellery and scarves; and amongst the tangle on the floor, her framed music certificates as though she had just been looking at them, her lock-up diary with she daren't imagine what outpourings crammed into its pages, and scrapbooks with cuttings from her magazines. Harriet would stand there wistfully day-dreaming, thinking: ah, how it could have been if Natasha was a girl like other girls. What it could have been like.

The police brought her home one day. She had been caught with a gang throwing bricks through the window of a show house on an exclusive development. And from this school, too, she was suspended for three weeks, found smoking pot.

'Where did you get it?' Harriet demanded wildly.

'Wouldn't you like to know?' came the retort.

She booked an appointment for them both at the child guidance clinic on the recommendation of her doctor, and for the duration of their session Natasha uttered not a word, except once, to chant, 'La-di-da-di-da'; while Harriet blundered her way through the half hour, saying nothing of pertinence and becoming more and more garrulous.

Natasha ran away to avoid their second appointment. She was gone for twenty-four hours.

'Where were you?' Harriet caught her daughter by the shoulders when she reappeared as if nothing were amiss, weeping with relief and rage.

The girl wrenched herself free. 'What do you care?' she countered, and disappeared to her room.

Harriet yearned for Oliver. Instead she was obliged to

confide in the doctor who had recommended the child guidance clinic. He commiserated with her and told her with false optimism, 'She'll more than likely grow out of it. It's probably just a phase. It's an attention-seeking age.'

'But it's not just that. She's always been like it, only not this bad. You've no idea how wearing it is. I feel like a piece – a piece of detritus. Completely worn down. She's so – She's cruel.'

'Believe me, I sympathise.'

'And I haven't any idea what she gets up to. She's three years under age, so I can't talk to her about the pill, but for all I know she may be sleeping around. I just don't know what to do.'

'You could go to the clinic on your own. It would still be beneficial.'

'It wouldn't be. There's no point . . . Do you know what it's like, to wish sometimes you didn't have a daughter, and then to despise yourself for your thoughts, so that you go overboard to make it up to her?'

'I really would recommend you saw someone. It would help you examine things from another aspect. It would help you just to air your problems.'

'No. Not without Natasha.'

She was suddenly annoyed. Then she noticed his doctor's ringed eyes. He had a dozen other patients to see during the course of the day. What could he do about one wayward girl, and a mother who was too inept to deal with her?

Her moods vacillated from day to day. She was disenchanted with her job at the foundation year college. At first she had enjoyed the lively atmosphere, the high spirits of the pupils and teachers alike; and the abundance of budding talent had excited her. But now she was tired of these students to whom she could no more relate than she could her daughter, with their bizarre clothes and hairstyles; the swearing and smoking. It had been different in her time, she thought. Or had it been? Wasn't that the grouse of every older generation? Perhaps the fault lay with her: she was intimidated by noise and over-exuberance and loutishness. And she disliked the pretensions of most modern art, which the college encouraged.

Sometimes she regretted moving to London and pined for the old house, wishing that she were surrounded by the security of memories after all. She contemplated the next forty years and wondered how she would endure them. But then she would go into her studio and take solace in there.

Once a week she visited her parents; she would sit on the rug, leaning her head against her father's wasted knees and holding his veined, freckled hand, feeling the energy-charged currents coursing between them as though her strength were being communicated to him. From the other room her mother carried on shouted conversations, quoting the newspapers, the bible, the vicar's last sermon, the woman up the road. Everything was vicarious; she was devoid of original ideas. Harriet thought her mother was daunted by the real world.

An invitation landed on her doormat for a ball in aid of cancer research. She threw it in the bin and posted a cheque; she would not dance for what Oliver had died of. And she imagined the guests whirling around a grand ballroom as in a Tissot painting; and in contrast her husband lying in bed, bald as a new-born baby.

She went out with men again and didn't speak of her past, having come to understand the susceptible male ego. In return for meals at restaurants and visits to the threatre she provided them with an interested and sympathetic ear; a woman who asked nothing of them and never criticised, and whom they shied away from knowing. It was a fair exchange; she shied away from their beds. Once she was almost tricked. After dinner out, she returned with a man to his house, to discover it was one of those mock creations whose facade was adorned with a token from every period. Inside, the sitting room was dominated by a large cocktail cabinet. Belatedly she noticed his shoes: they were fringed and buckled and tassled. Oliver had maintained you could tell a man by his shoes. She left abruptly.

She stopped going out, but nightly had erotic dreams from which she awoke on the point of orgasm. She would lie there feeling skin on skin, an anonymous penis stirring within her, so aroused she could not get back to sleep. She resorted to doing it to herself. So-lonely Harriet, ashamed of her needs, ashamed that she was surviving; and striving to retain the link with Oliver.

'You must screw with the next man who takes you out,' said Astrid, never one to mince words.

'For God's sake,' Harriet said, exasperated, 'I don't want to. Won't you get that into your head?' She still shuddered to think of her sordid experience in Devon.

'You won't bring Oliver back to life by being chaste.'

'You bitch.'

A week passed without their speaking; then she received a card from Astrid: 'I was only trying to drag you out of it, in my own clumsy way. Love you to the bitter end (may it not be too bitter).'

They met for lunch and fell into each other's arms like old lovers. Astrid, noticing Harriet's lit-up eyes and upward-tilted mouth, said, 'You've done it.'

'Done what?' asked Harriet, smile dying. 'Oh for God's sake, is that all you think of?'

'But you've got your illuminated look. It's not my fault if I jump to the wrong conclusion.' She turned as she spoke, to strike up eye-contact with a man sitting at the bar.

Harriet told her friend's swivelled head, 'I'm giving up my job. I'm going freelance. Taking commissions. And I'm going to teach classes at home in my studio.'

She received nearly thirty replies to the advertisement

she and Astrid composed, and handed in her resignation at college with relief, feeling for the first time since Oliver's death that she was in charge of her own life.

One of the men who applied to attend her Saturday class, starting in September, was called Elliot Grainger.

The eighth principal event of Harriet's adult life.

10

The day before Gnat's fourteenth birthday. She dreads it. Being here. Last year Dimple had come to stay, and they had had their quarrel.

Dear Dimple, she writes in her head, on the loo, in the bath, lying in bed.

Well I daresay this letter will come as a bit of a surprise to you. I mean we didn't exactly hit it off last time we saw each other, did we? though I guess that was my fault, and I've really been thinking about you a lot and trying to work things out in my head. Well, and there's other people trying to work things out for me also. You see something awful happened – it was me – I did something awful and they put me in a special place for disturbed kids, called Turner's End. It sounds dreadful, doesn't it? But actually you get used to it and it does help sort things out in your head in a way. I mean at first I just wanted to yell at everyone. I don't anymore.

I don't really know what to write, or what you think of me now, but I've been going crazy (hah!) with thoughts about how we were blood-sisters, and the laughs we had, and when we stayed at each other's houses and yapped all night, and made shapes on the wall in the torchlight, and riding in the Great Park. And I know I was to blame for that weekend in London. I just felt bad being reminded of everything I'd left behind. I was jealous of you and I felt all screwed up inside, you having everything the way I wanted it. I missed Daddy so much and I kept thinking about other birthdays when he'd been around, and I had to pretend I didn't care about anything so as to make it easier, if you see what I mean.

So things aren't too great, what with me stuck here, and I've made my mother hate me, so I don't know if I can ever go home, and it's my birthday tomorrow. It'll be really weird. But you know what? Inside me I feel kind of different, even from when you and I were friends. I've done so much talking and crying and thinking, it's like my insides have been turned outwards if you see what I mean. I've started playing the cello again and I've decided that one day I'm going to play in an orchestra. I want to be a proper musician, like Jacqueline du Prè. That's my goal. So I'll have to get into music college. I've decided, and that makes me happy. It gives me something special to think about and I know I can do it.

I've made some friends here. There's one girl called Maria I'm friends with particularly. She's older than me and very pretty with hair that makes me sick with jealousy, but she's really screwed up and I'm really sorry for her. She doesn't know what will happen to her. And there's a boy called Robert who I like a hell of a lot, but that's all a bit muddled and I'm playing it a bit cool at the moment. I also still sometimes think of a boy called Phillip and maybe I'm in love with him too. At first I thought I was with Dr Middleton, the psychiatrist who's been helping me, but I'm not after all. He knows everything in the world about me. Robert's going home soon. Lucky thing. He says when I get out he'll take me to the flicks. You see, it was me who got him to talk again, but it's too complicated to explain. Actually, I could really make you laugh with some of the goings-on in this place. I mean, it's sad, but sometimes it's really funny. I read a lot too. I read a fantastic book called *The Prophet* the other day three times all the way through. Maybe you wouldn't like it. We like different books and things. Maybe I've become too different for you to like me anymore. I mean, such a lot has happened and I'm not the same me. I feel like I've travelled the world and back and I've got all these things inside me, all these experiences. Sometimes I feel old. Not a girl anymore. It's a funny feeling. I cry about that. Maybe I've become wet.

Please write. I'm really sorry for the way I was. I mean you were my best friend and I loused it up.

How's school? How are your parents? Do you still ride? By the way your short hair didn't make you look fat. It was really nice. How tall are you? I'm still small. And I hate my boobs. But I guess I'm lumbered with them, so there's no point in griping.

Well I guess that's all. I mean I could go on forever, there's so much to tell you. I could write pages, a book even.

I hope you'll be my friend again.

Lots of love, Gnat.

In her mind's eye she adds a row of kisses, draws a picture of herself with an arrow pointing to her nose, saying 'stud gone,' draws a horse, and a heart. In her mind she folds the letter, puts it in an envelope, addresses it and takes it to the post.

But she is actually in bed. It is the middle of the night, and she never commits pen to paper. Too much has happened.

• • •

The day before Natasha's birthday, and little more than a year after her first Saturday class, here she is in the psychiatrist's fresh-smelling room, sharing her turbulent memories with him, drawing nearer that fateful evening which put her daughter in Turner's End. Elliot still loyal to her, still wanting to marry her.

'I'll never forget that first class in my own studio,' Harriet says. 'God, it was nerve-wracking. But I emerged entire. It was elating, that sense of my own worth and achievement afterwards.'

She had cleared the conservatory of half the plants and everyone took their places quietly in the chairs arranged in a semi-circle. A couple of people had brought easels; all had brought drawing pads, pencils and putty-rubbers, as she'd instructed. No charcoal or paints that first time. Harriet provided three easels and had spare materials available. She'd practised her initial patter as though it were the Prime Minister's inaugural speech for the past week, beaming in front of the long mirror in her bedroom; but when the time came her mouth was so frozen she could coax only the tiniest smile from it. She could barely speak, confronted by these seven expectant adults, and found herself longing for her class of boisterous teenagers. How conceited to imagine she had anything to offer, that anyone should wish to heed her.

What can I tell them?

And the Lord said unto them; her mother's pious voice reading from the bible suddenly rang in her head, and nervous laughter threatened to burst from her.

'Good morning –' She listened to her own tremulous tones bouncing off the glass walls of the conservatory. 'I'm so glad to see you've all made it –' And here a numerical check obliged her to glance at each of them, and her eyes alighted on a tall man whose grave eyes met hers. She turned away quickly and went on, 'I hope that besides enjoying ourselves we can impart some knowledge to each other. Now, to begin with, this first morning, I just want to see the sort of standard you're at. It's vital that apart from learning the craft, the technique of drawing and using colour, you express yourselves, your own individuality. No one else's. Least of all mine.'

Pause, breathe. And Harriet was astonished to see that they were really listening; interested in what *she* had to say.

They set to work, drawing the still life she had set up on a small wicker table: jug, bowl, knife, apple, loaf of bread; and presently there issued from the room those sounds she loved – pencils scratching against paper, impatient rubbing out, pencils shading, pencils being sharpened, fingers rubbing on the paper, sighs, frustrated exclamations, breathing burdened with concentration, whispers between strangers no longer strangers. Contact made here in this room. And she felt proud, so proud.

She studied her seven pupils: three middle-aged women somewhere between forty-five and sixty-five, homely, ordinary; one younger, enormously fat in a tent-like dress, her face tumbling into wedges of flesh. The men: one elderly, broken-veined big nose; another insipid and beige with an anxious expression; and finally the dark-eyed man with the narrow, sensitive face. He smiled up at her over his drawing board, and she was embarrassed that once again he'd caught her looking at him.

She herself sketched the still life for a while, then she got up to see how the class was progressing. The three middle-aged women were all beginners and she explained to them the importance of seeing the shapes and angles made between the different objects, and the inter-relationship between the objects themselves, making use of the curves, the points; explaining that one actually did not see what one thought one saw. The fat woman seemed to be doing well, apart from making the knife too long and thin, and she basked in Harriet's gentle encouragement.

She was beginning to enjoy herself, to relax. Onto the men: the old one drew with a miniaturist's eye and was too fussy in his approach; the beige man, as she had suspected, lacked confidence and had used too many strokes besides having no feel for proportion. She told him about the need to see the still life as an entirety and uniting the subjects more simply, as a fluid design. She left the tall dark man called Elliot Grainger until last. He was good, using assured, swift strokes and somehow she felt cheated.

'You're obviously a pro,' she said, bending over his drawing.

He looked up, amused. 'Not exactly.' A deep voice; slightly lopsided smile, slightly crooked front tooth. His eyes were inside hers.

She retreated to her place and continued with her own sketching, but was unable to concentrate.

The two and a half hours passed. Harriet announced that the following Saturday they would be having a model and could use colour if they wished. Everyone looked pleased. They paid her and left. All of them. She thought about Elliot Grainger the entire week. In between Oliver's face reproached her.

Saturday came round again and he had not turned up; and for Harriet it was as though her day had lost its purpose.

He arrived ten minutes late when she had given up, and her spirits soared.

'Sorry I'm late, but look what I've got. I had to clean it up. I was walking the dog in Richmond Park and suddenly saw it.'

He delved into a holdall and laid a magnificent antler on the table. She touched it sadly.

'What's wrong?' he asked, concerned. 'I thought I'd leave it here. We could draw it sometime.'

'It's perfect to draw.'

'Isn't it beautiful? Pure sculpture.'

'Yes. But would the stag have died?'

The rest of the class, concentrating on the recumbent model, holding up rulers in the air, squinting and peering . . .

'No,' he said. 'This was most likely lying around from last spring. And even if it had happened in a fight it wouldn't cause the stag's death. Don't look so upset,' he said softly. 'Nature has it all worked out.'

'Yes I know.'

He lingered for a moment then went over to the remaining free chair and took out his materials from an artist's box. Harriet watched him covertly. His actions were leisurely and relaxed; there was nothing harrassed or nervous about him. She noticed the way he sat – slightly sideways on – at his easel, the angle of his arm as he worked, and how he held the charcoal. He was engrossed, and the pleasure on his face was obvious. She wondered how old he was, and thought probably younger than her. Was he married? The thought only then occurred to her, and she was unreasonably depressed because she knew he was bound to be married.

She did the rounds of the class, and this time when she came to him she was glad to see he had not accurately proportioned the woman's body. This enabled her to show off. She was aware she was doing it. She was like a pleased child.

He stayed behind at the end, ostensibly to help her clear away. She pretended to be unsurprised and take for granted his assistance. But she was so conscious of him; it was like a thickness in the air. She prickled with it. They folded her easels, moved chairs, unplugged the fan heater, put the various materials in a drawer, doing everything in silence, together, until the room was straight. And still he lingered. She felt shy and ungainly. The back of her neck was hot.

For a moment he appraised her, like a surgeon about to make an incision, she thought, then his face buckled into its crooked smile. She smiled back.

Say something intelligent Harriet. 'Where—'

'– You're an excellent teacher.'

They spoke at the same time and laughed self-consciously.

'You're just saying that.' She pushed her fringe away from her forehead.

'I'm not. Why should I? You apply psychology. And you give. Too many people simply instruct. You give.'

'Thank you. That's kind of you.'

'I'm not saying it to be kind. Can I take you out to lunch?'

'I—'

Her daughter, black-clad, hair spiked with gel, stud in nose, storming into the conservatory, assuming her mother to be on her own.

'I'm going out. I'll be staying the night.'

'Where?' Harriet asked.

Natasha looked warily from her mother to the man.

'Where?' Harriet repeated, trying to sound authorative.

'What does it matter, for Christ's sake? I've done my prep. Vicky's if you must know.'

And out she went, leaving the door open and switching her ghetto blaster on top volume; casting a backward, flirtatious glance at Elliot Grainger.

'My daughter,' Harriet apologised, touching the corner of her trembling mouth.

'Lunch,' he said, steering her from the room.

He introduced her to his car. 'The love of my life.'

'Not your wife?' she asked guilessly.

'I'm divorced,' he said, sounding amused, 'if that's what you're trying to ascertain. Amicably,' he added. 'No children. So now we've covered that one.'

She huddled into her seat, miserable at her own gaucheness.

'And you?'

'My husband died.'

She waited for the change of subject.

'I think we have a lot of talking to do,' he said gently.

Dog hairs drifted around, settling on her clothes. An elderly labrador was responsible, he told her. As he drove he would occasionally turn to look at her; again when the car was stationary at some lights: a faintly quizzical frown.

'I'm taking you into the dark depths of the wrong part of Battersea,' he said. 'Do you mind?'

'The Dog's Home?'

'If you like. But I had somewhere else in mind. The most special place in London, in fact.'

Why her? Why should he be interested enough in her to take her somewhere special? She was both jubilant and confused, could not believe he would sustain his interest in her for long, particularly having met Natasha.

They passed rows of terraced houses set back from filthy pavements; children playing in the road, scuffling and shrieking. 'Oi, that hurt,' she heard a boy cry out; a woman in a man's brown coat, shuffling along, trailing a shopping basket on wheels. And at the zebra crossing an old crippled man took forever, and she suffered for him. A child walked behind him, aping his movements grotesquely. Elliot was suffering also; she could tell. He stared fixedly ahead and neither of them said anything; but they were intrinsically bound by the poignant vignette. His hand tightened on the gear stick and she resisted the urge to cover it with hers.

A dog hair flew into her eye and she exclaimed loudly.

'What is it?'

'I'm sorry. Just a dog hair in my eye.'

'Don't apologise, for Christ's sake.'

He pulled over to the kerb, ignoring the hooting behind him. 'Let me see.'

'No, really—'

'Yes.'

'I can do it.'

'Ah, but I'm an expert.'

'How come?' Happy. Her eye sore and beginning to run. But she was asurdedly happy.

'I wrote a thesis once, entitled, The Relevance and Usage of Dog Hairs Lodged in the Human Eyeball. It was regarded as a major breakthrough in research.'

'Oh Elliot, really!'

'You mustn't laugh because your eyes crinkle up and I won't find it. Keep still.'

He held her face with his right hand, and with his left, prised her lids apart, peering deeply into her eye.

'Found it.'

Delicately he drew out the hair, and she blinked, relieved. His fingers caressed her cheekbone briefly then moved away. Flustered, she failed to think of something light-hearted to say, and no further conversation was exchanged until he finally parked outside a dismal parade of shops in a street no different to the others they'd passed.

'We're here.'

He opened a glass-paned front door, pushed aside the beaded curtain behind it and led her into the most unique place of her life. She gazed, enchanted, about her, at the extraordinary amalgam of curios and mementos cluttering shelves, walls and even the ceiling. Nothing matched; assorted chairs were painted clashing colours, and tables were propped up on blocks of wood to stabilise them. Harriet commented that it was kitsch, but then thought that that was not the appropriate word. Edith Piaf's voice was soft in the background; the pungent odours of garlic and olive oil, rosemary and red wine instantly invoked hot-summer-holiday recollections.

Elliot said, 'A pearl in the middle of Battersea.'

'It's absolutely amazing,' she said, her eyes everywhere at once.

Jossi Lenski, the owner and ex-boxer, came over to them:

huge, monkey-faced beneath cropped black hair. He kissed Elliot on either cheek. Elliot introduced Harriet.

'She,' Jossi observed in his gutteral Polish accent, 'is something.'

'I know,' agreed Elliot.

Harriet, unable to stop grinning, accepted the menu from Jossi. He handed it to her like a priest passing her a bible. Other customers arriving, appearing through the beads like merry Rastafarians. Impossible to believe that just outside, defeated women pushed their baskets full of products bought by coupons, children fought in the streets and men brawled in pubs. She sipped her wine, and felt Elliot staring at her again.

'What do you think of it?' he asked.

'It's wonderful. A cross between Eastern Europe – not that I've ever been – and Montmartre. I wish I could paint atmosphere. Just the atmosphere, in vibrant colours.'

'Why don't you?'

'I did once –' Remembering: after Oliver's affair with C, those lonely explosions of colour on canvas. '– I even won a prize for some competition. But essentially I'm a realist. Perhaps I'm boring.' She knew the wine was affecting her.

'Now you'll make me angry.'

Jossi reappeared, bearing two plates heaped with seafood tagliatelli tossed in cream, parmesan resting on top like soft dust. He set down a bowl of hot garlic bread on the table, kissed his fingers with a smacking noise and left them.

More wine. Shadows prancing on and off Harriet's flushed cheekbones.

'You're—' Elliot didn't complete the sentence.

She smiled at him questioningly and he shook his head.

'I'll tell you one day.'

One day. He spoke of the future. Casually? Or with meaning? He was bound to let her down. She thought she was drunk; couldn't eat.

'Please don't stare at me like that.'

'I'm sorry. You're very stareable-at-able.'

He was not touching his food either. Later he joked that they could each have had a single whitebait on their plates and wouldn't have noticed.

'I – you're a good artist,' she said. 'Have you done much painting before?'

'In a way. I'm an architect. But I want to know about you. Everything. What about your husband? Can you speak about him? When did he die?'

All those times when she had wanted to talk about Oliver and was not permitted to – and now he was locked within her. She was afraid to bring him out, that in speaking of him she would alienate Elliot. There again, part of her was reluctant to share Oliver, to have a stranger encroach on his territory, threatening that link which the passing years were doing their utmost to erode.

She didn't answer.

'Can't you talk about it yet?'

His warm tone punctured her with its tenderness, and her eyes swam.

'Harriet? Oh, Harriet, I'm sorry.'

He reached across the table to cradle her head, and in the middle of Lenski's restaurant, the first time since that day her bathroom radiator had spouted water, she wept.

She went to the lavatory, weed out her two glasses of wine, splashed water on her face, brushed her hair, put on more scarlet lipstick, and re-emerged into the restaurant. The tagliatelli had gone. In its place were thin escalopes of salmon. Harriet started to talk. And the salmon grew cold also. Elliot grasped her hand throughout. Elliot, with whom she refused to go to bed for two months because of Oliver and when she did, wept for hours afterwards; with whom she tried to finish a couple of times because he was severing the Thread; who would surely tire of her, but who has remained constant, been endlessly understanding of her moods of despair, doubts, guilt, and all the many dramas with Natasha; has accepted the whole package; and who is, unbelievably, still there.

• • •

'Last night I dreamed I was going out with a skinhead,' Gnat tells Dr Middleton, 'but my mother didn't approve so I had to hide him in my bed. I told him he could stay there as long as he liked satay sauce. Can you imagine! Anyway, he doesn't, so up he gets – he's wearing boxer shorts with skeletons on them, and a football shirt – and goes to my mother's car. And Brett Anderson from the group Suede is there, holding my cello. I'm there too, and so's my mother, with Pirate on her lap. She asks the skinhead how many GCSEs he's got and he says one in woodwork, and she slaps him on the back, telling him how clever he is and that she's always wanted to learn woodwork. I mean, isn't it hysterical? So, then he becomes old and he's Tom, and we're all driving off in Elliot's car to picnic by the river in Windsor. It wasn't bad as dreams go. I woke up giggling. Properly giggling. Ripples inside me like tiny slivers of silver water . . .

'I remember the swallows we had in our garden in Windsor,' she says, propelled by her mercurial chain of thoughts. 'They nested in the same place each year, beneath the roof gutter. And there were always swallows by the river in summer. They'd swoop onto the water, just skimming its surface. I loved to watch them. I wish I were a swallow. I wish I could be a swallow for my birthday tomorrow. For a day.'

She becomes pensive and blinks in the sharp sunlight which penetrates the room. She wonders how his new baby is, wonders about his life, his home, his wife, his son. Do they ever yell at each other?

'I mean I don't know who I am anymore,' she mumbles. 'I don't know me.'

'Do you think you did before you came here?'

'I don't know.'

'The trouble is, Gnat, the "me" you refer to is made up of many components. Some have to be nurtured.' A weighty pause, a significant look, then, 'Can you tell me a bit about when your mother started going out with Elliot?'

She remembers her mother humming as she cooked for three people again, that light shining out from inside her as though nothing could hurt her, and herself wanting to hurt her, to destroy her serenity, jealous of it and afraid of something nameless.

At mealtimes they tried to include her in conversation and she would talk across Harriet and flirt blatantly with Elliot. She'd taken to wearing metallic blue lipstick and on one occasion she grabbed his napkin, planted blue kisses on it, then handed it back. When Ben Elton was on television they watched him together and she laughed extra loudly so Harriet – who disliked him – would hear.

Her mother, smelling of Body Shop Musk, preparing to go out; making herself beautiful for Elliot. The baby-sitter arriving.

'I don't need a baby-sitter. It's wet. How do you think I feel having a baby-sitter.'

'It's against the law for a child under fourteen to be left alone in the house. You know it is,' Harriet told her in her weary voice, lifting her fingers to her temples as she did when she couldn't face a scene.

'I'm not a child.'

'You are in the eyes of the law.'

She found an orange tunic at the Sue Ryder shop. It was meant to have a blouse under it but she wore nothing, and her breasts bulged at the sides. She adhered a body sticker to her upper arm, donned black boots and black tights, and spiked her hair. Elliot was taking them out for dinner. Her attire was solely for him.

Her mother was appalled. 'You can't go out like that.'

'Yes I can.'

'You can't. You look ridiculous. You look like a child prostitute.'

Goading her, Gnat leaned against the wall suggestively and crossed one leg over the other. 'Fuck me, babe,' she drawled, as she'd heard a prostitute drawl in a film, and pretended to smoke a cigarette.

Harriet's patience snapped and she screamed, 'I've had enough. I've had it up to *here*—' She drew a line above her head.

And Gnat laughed at her, dancing around her manically, chanting, 'I'm a child prostitute. I'm a child prostitute. Fuck me. Fuck me.'

Her mother ran upstairs to her room, slamming the door behind her.

'And how did you feel then?' Dr Middleton asks.

Gnat looks sheepishly at him. 'Mostly I was glad, because I had one of my black moods, and I was just so cross with her. I was a bit sorry I think. But you see, inside me I was screwed-up and I think it bugged me she didn't try to find out. I feel bad about it now though.'

'Why?'

'I've made her hate me.'

In the end she wore a black tee-shirt underneath the tunic because Elliot said it was cold and he didn't want her to be ill. She was ill anyway; so upset seeing the gooey way they stared at each other at the restaurant, that she ate everything in sight: the long, thin stick things on which she plastered butter, rolls, a starter, a main course, and strawberries and cream to finish, besides half of Elliot's crème brulée. Back home she was sick. Even in her misery and pain she was intrigued to notice that the strawberries were still whole.

'Can you remember any good times since your father died?' Dr Middleton asks.

'Sundays,' Gnat answers without hesitation, in a tone of intense longing.

The three of them cramming into Harriet's car, as well as Elliot's old labrador and their spaniel. Walking in Richmond Park, she on one side of Elliot, Harriet the other. Arms linked. Running down hills. Laughter. Yes, laughter. I love you, Elliot. I'm going to marry you when I'm old enough. Pulling him away from her mother, pretending to punch him, and him lifting her into the air. The deer grazing unperturbed, looking up intermittently, forelegs pointed, wet noses quivering.

Sundays. The smell of a roast in the Aga. Crisp potatos, carrots done in layers with pine nuts. On Sundays she cleaned out Rodent Mark 2's cage. She played with him (it, her), and watched him on his wheel, going round in one direction then the other, tireless, his claws working frantically. She photographed him and won a junior competition with a close-up of Rodent Mark 2's nose, whiskers and eyes.

On Sundays she wrote pages in her lock-up diary: a torrent of rage and agony. She wore the key on a string round her neck. She listened to her favourite tapes and wrote down the words; drew pictures of Sting and Bowie; cut up clothes; sorted out her jewellery and beads; smoked by the open window if she had any fags. She had used to practise her cello; but she was off the cello. It was wet. Besides, she'd cut the strings to stop her mother nagging at her to play.

'I overheard Elliot saying something to my mother,' she recalls. 'He said, "She is in search of her identity." I didn't think about it much then, but it stuck in my head, and I guess he meant me, didn't he?'

'Did your relationship with your daughter deteriorate after you started going out with Elliot?'

'I don't know that it deteriorated,' Harriet muses. 'It was already at an all-time low. It changed; acquired another dimension. We hadn't been competitive as two *women* before. Now we were rivals as women. It was a more adult battle, and I suppose the more serious for it. I think everything was leading up to some kind of crisis. Thank God Elliot is not one of those men with a Lolita complex.'

The difficulties of adjusting to a new relationship, learning the habits of a different partner, growing to trust him, coming to terms with her guilt over Oliver – and simultaneously juggling with the unpredictable moods of her daughter.

'At first she refused to speak to Elliot. She found a drawerful of photos of Oliver, and displayed them prominently all round the house, just before Elliot arrived one evening. I remember what he said – let's face it, he could hardly ignore them – 'Good looking chap,' he said. You should have seen Natasha's expression. She was stunned; the wind completely taken out of her sails. And then one day I went into my studio to find the portrait I was doing of him smeared with red paint. Other canvases also. It was horrific. Like some ghastly voodoo ritual. Red paint like blood everywhere.' Her voice quavers and she clears her throat. 'I didn't know what to do. Sometimes I thought I'd go demented. I found my daughter's vindictiveness towards me quite, quite terrifying. Nobody could offer me help or advice. She was trying to destroy my chance of happiness.'

Trembling with pent-up rage, all she said to her daughter was, 'How would you like it if I desecrated your possessions or ruined your work you'd spent ages over and was important to you?'

Natasha yelled back, 'You're being unfair to Daddy. And I hate you.'

What would have happened, Harriet wonders now, if at that point she had taken her child in her arms?

As it became apparent Elliot was not about to disappear but was establishing himself as a fixture in their lives, the girl's attitude towards him altered and just as she had done with her father, she vied for his affection, and Harriet was truly afraid.

She returned to the doctor, who again recommended therapy. She explained – again – her daughter would not attend, and he tried to convince her to go on her own. She requested Valium instead. He refused. Please, she begged him. I think I'm going crazy. She's wrecking my life, my relationship. He made sympathetic 'tch-tch' sounds, and she went away despondent and resentful, with no prescription and a few empty words. She thought she could not take any more.

Elliot comforting her. Making love to her. Watching themselves in the mirror; they were beautiful together. She could forget everything. But it was always there, waiting: punishment for remission.

One evening after dinner she related her latest quarrel with her daughter to him.

He said, 'She is in search of her identity.'

Then she turned and, with a pang of conscience, saw Natasha standing in the doorway.

Harriet reaches for the glass of water on the table. Her head aches. People compliment her that she looks ten years younger than her age, and she cannot understand why she doesn't look old. Sometimes there is a line to the left of her mouth, a sabre curve from her nostril to the edge of her lips. She becomes ultra conscious of it, thinks that it's exaggeratedly deep and that she's ugly and haggard because of it; she can feel it dragging her mouth downwards, and sits in front of the mirror smoothing it with rueful fingertips.

'I realise now that my daughter was crying out for help,' she says. 'Do you know Beethoven's fourth piano concerto?'

'Yes.' The psychiatrist raises amused eyebrows.

'That second movement always reminds me of Gnat and myself. The altercation between piano and orchestra. First the orchestra in ascendence, then as it dies away, the piano.'

'You called her Gnat.'

'Did I?' She has some more water. 'What does that mean?'

'Can you tell me?'

'Oh God. If you knew what an effort all this is. The concentration. I'm continually drained. Sometimes I feel I've nothing left of myself to give.'

'I know.'

'You never criticise me.'

'That's not my job.'

'Will I always blame myself?'

'Blame doesn't come into this. I've told you.'

She sighs – and as the water sticks in her gullet, gives a small 'hic'.

'I want her to be happy. I really do. And I want *me* to be happy. I've got just as much right as her.'

'You called her Gnat,' he repeats.

'Yes. Yes. Perhaps I've got rid of a lot of the anger.'

He nods.

'I'm so sorry for her. She's probably suffered more than me over the years, after all, the demon has been living inside *her*. Potentially she's a loveable girl. She has many loveable traits . . . I care.'

He nods again.

'Perhaps I'm seeing her as her own self, respecting her for that. Perhaps I'm relating more to her.'

'Ah. Now that *is* important.'

'Tomorrow's her fourteenth birthday. I keep thinking of her, my child, *my* child, on her own in that place for her fourteenth birthday. Oh I'm sorry. What a mess I am. I'm always crying. Such a mess. Are all your patients like this? You poor man! I don't know how you keep sane . . . It's just the thought of her having her birthday in that place. In an adolescent home, for God's sake.'

• • •

Her fourteenth birthday. Who would have thought she'd spend it in a place for loopy kids? At breakfast she receives several presents, and cards from everyone including the staff. Robert has given her back the jumping beans and also a tiny glass hedgehog. He looks on in embarrassment as she peels away the Sellotape and paper.

'C-careful. It's fra-fra-gile.'

'It's lovely,' she says when she finally gets to it, wanting to cry, wanting to kiss him, but not here in front of everyone. Jason starts to give her his card, then won't let go of it.

'Don't you want me to have it then?' Gnat says; and he unclenches his fist so that the crumpled card drops to the floor.

While she is bent down, retrieving it he envelopes her in a hug, making odd, grunting noises, and she panics. 'No Jason,' she shouts, lashing out. 'Let me go.' She can smell his nasty breath.

'Jason,' she hears The Spoon say quietly; and he releases her, shamefaced. And she is shamed, realises he was demonstrating affection in the only way he knew. She has failed him and herself.

She gives him a quick kiss. 'Thank you, Jason.'

The Spoon hands her three more cards. Gnat recognises the writing: two are from her mother, one Elliot. Dry-mouthed, she opens his. On the front is a picture of a girl with a sunhat reading under a tree, a puppy on her lap. Inside he has put, 'Lots and lots of love to my favourite –' and has drawn a Gnat where her name should be.

The next one is from Rodent Mark 2 and the spaniel, and Harriet has done cartoon drawings which make her smile fleetingly, before her throat constricts.

She opens the third and reads the cryptic printed message – 'Happy birthday from someone you can reach' – several times, varying the emphasis so that the meaning is altered.

In the dormitory she arranges the cards on the chest of drawers and bedside locker, and reads her mother's again in case she has missed something. The single X. Then she goes to put on her charm bracelet. It is gone from the little bowl where she is certain she placed it.

'My bracelet,' she shrieks. 'Who's taken my bracelet?'

She runs from one girl to the other, grabbing each in turn.

Alice, fixing her hair in a pony-tail, pushes her aside. 'Bugger off, I'm fed up with you,' she says.

'Don't look at me,' shrugs Maria, who's making her bed.

'Who took it?' Gnat shouts, running back and forth frenziedly.

'What's happened?' The Spoon's kind face peeps round the door.

'Someone's stolen the charm bracelet Mummy gave me.'

The nurse's eyes widen, and for a moment she is too astonished to say anything.

'Now why do you think someone's stolen it?' she asks after a second or two.

Unaware she referred to her mother as 'Mummy', Gnat says wildly, 'Well I put it in the bowl where I always put it, so they must've. I'll kill whoever's taken it. Honestly I will.' Red-faced, she twirls around on the spot and rocks on her heels.

'Now pet, you really must calm down. First we'll look for it in an organised way, then if we don't find it we'll do some inquiring.'

She calms slightly. 'I'm not going to lessons till I get it back.'

'That's fair enough.'

They begin their search: under all the beds, amongst the bedclothes, behind furniture, in the bathroom, amongst the dirty linen; and downstairs – everywhere they can think of. A host of other articles are unearthed during their quest, but not the bracelet.

'You see.' Gnat's tone is resigned. 'I told you someone had taken it. Everyone's a bloody thief in this dump.'

She bursts into sobs. It is surely a grim omen that she should have lost the charm bracelet on her fourteenth birthday. From now on her life will be a disaster. Everything will be a disaster, she knows it.

She sits on the window seat in the recreation room, scratching the eczema that has flared up on the inside of her wrist, looking out at the blustery autumnal day, the windswept trees scattering leaves, her blurred hill, the damp tennis court where a solitary rook guards the net; and her shoulders slump in desolation. She has been at Turner's End all her life; never known anything else; will never know anything else. The rook is sinister. She wishes it would fly off.

'I hate it,' she wails. 'I hate everything. Just when you think things are going right, they go wrong. I mean what's the point? What's the bloody point of me doing my cello, and trying to sort things? I mean what'll *happen* to me?'

'Hush pet.' The Spoon lays a placatory hand on her arm.

'I want my bracelet.'

'I'm sure we'll find it. When you undressed last night did you go directly to bed?'

'I had a bath. But it's not in the bathroom. We searched there.'

'I know we did. Did you wear a dressing-gown to go in there?'

Gnat's expression changing, lightening.

'Yes.'

'Do you think there's a chance—'

Her sentence is left suspended as Gnat charges upstairs to the dormitory. Her dressing-gown is hanging with several others on the the hook on the door, and she fumbles in the pocket; the silver charm bracelet meets her fingers. She squeals with relief and joy, dances around. 'I found it. I found it.' Then, suddenly weak, sinks onto the bed and buries her head between her knees. The bracelet dangles from her hand. For a while longer she remains there, then she gets up and goes to her lessons, in subdued mood.

Tea. They have attempted to make some sort of party for her. The dining room has been decorated with streamers and balloons on which they have written, in fluorescent felt-pen, 'Happy birthday Gnat;' the tables are festively laid with red paper cloths and crackers, and there is a decent assortment of biscuits as well as a birthday cake.

Seeing the room like this takes her back to countless children's teaparties she attended as a little girl, and she wonders what happened to the children she used to know. She cuts the cake and wishes. To go home. She pulls a cracker with Dr Middleton who is on one side of her, and with Robert on the other. They don their hats and someone sets Gnat's on her head. Her cheeks ache from her forced, fixed grin. Jason is licking his plate, and Alice, with her 'blue' phobia, is staring mesmerised at Susan's blue jumper. 'You put it on on purpose,' she hisses.

Lisa is missing from the table, disappeared into thin air

through the unlocked doors, her uneven legs taken flight. Rumour has it the fire in the farm barn down the road was started by her. Rumour also has it she's done herself in, that her body was found on the railway line. Who knows? No one knows anything for sure here. It's all a mega trick.

Gnat wishes she'd been nicer to her.

Robert nudges her. 'If we put s-ome mu-music on we could d-da-dance.'

'I don't know. I don't feel like dancing.'

'Spoilsp-sp-sport.'

'I'm not. I'm just not in the mood. And everybody'd be watching.'

He sits back, nettled, then tries again. 'You're ever s-so pr-pretty,' he mumbles.

And she perks up slightly. 'Do you really think so?'

'Yes. Tha-that's why I s-s-s-said it, d-dope.'

He has begun to tease her lately, become more manly, masterful.

'Well I still don't feel like dancing.' She looks away from him.

'Wh-what do you f-feel like then?' he asks, peeved.

Give us a feel, the boys said at her school. And she let them. She doesn't want to see them ever again. None of them. And how will she face them as if nothing's happened? She can hear them jeering; the kids she had pretended were friends. Cruel laughter. Laughter that was invariably at someone's expense. Once she said to Elliot, 'You're laughing at me.' 'No,' he corrected her. 'I'm laughing with you.'

'I feel like thinking,' she tells Robert.

'Are you f-feeling bad?'

'I *am* bad,' she replies fiercely. 'Bad, bad, bad.' She springs up and goes from the room, outside, into the garden.

Leaning against the tennis net where earlier she had seen the rook, she rubs her arms to keep warm. The wind whips her hair across her mouth, and tendrils catch between her lips. She is bitterly disappointed in herself. She had thought she was improving, but this morning that old black rage had possessed her. I'll kill whoever's taken it. And certainly she had, in her frenzy, felt almost murderous. She thinks of the rook; remembers the word, iniquitous, meaning evil. The rook was evil. She is evil. And unloveable. Nobody will ever love her. Her father loved her. Would he love her as she was now?

I hate myself.

The wind lashes at the tennis net, at her clothes, her face, her memories. She recalls the time Harriet wanted to paint her, and she refused to comply.

'Please, Natasha. It's for a competition.'
'I don't care about some fucking competition.'
'Don't say that.'
'What?'
'What you just did.'
'You mean, fuck? Astrid says it. I've heard her. What's wrong with fuck, for fuck's sake? You do it. You do it with Elliot. Fuck, fuck, fuck, fuck, fuck.'
'Shut up. Get out. Go on. Get out. You're a monster.'

Her mother's face contorted. Gnat can visualise it, drained of colour and all twisted up, making her, briefly, ugly. And all she had wanted to do was paint her daughter. Such a small and reasonable request to make. Gnat couldn't even grant her that. And it would have been quite fun to see her portrait shoved on some wall.

I'm iniquitous.

And the time she was locked out. It was a Saturday night and she was at a girl's whose parents were away. The older brother had invited some friends over, and they sat round the TV, eating crisps, drinking beer and smoking. Someone had managed to acquire a pornographic video, and she watched in fascinated horror the sexual antics between a young woman, a goat and two men. The others found it hilarious: screeched with laughter, clapped, and imitated the antics with obscene gestures. She pretended to joke with them, and smoked a few puffs from a couple of joints that were offered around; but they made her feel worse. There was a whistling in her ears. A boy had his hands beneath her jumper, groping for her breasts, scratching them viciously and hurting them. He was ugly; had red wet lips, smelt of beer. The whistling became a piercing sound in her ears. She fought him and broke away – ran down interminable flights of stone steps in the tower block where each floor was the same and smelt of urine. Raised voices quarrelling or the television blaring out at top volume came from behind hostile doors. Her heart raced with her. Her breasts were sore from the boy's filthy nails raking her skin. And then she stopped in her flight: nobody was pursuing her; they were not bothered. They were far too immersed in their revelry, up all those flights of stairs, to be bothered by her.

It was past midnight; foggy, wintry night, the street lights casting a haze in the dank air. Gnat's head span from the pot and the beer, and with recurring images of the video. She could feel the spotty boy's rubbery lips on hers – and then was aware of footsteps behind her as she walked, becoming faster, running with her, alongside her; and abruptly ceasing. She realised they had been her own, echoing.

She had only ever visited her friend by bus. Everything looked different on foot, in the fog. She was lost, and afraid to ask the few people she saw. She was in the midst of a surreal nightmare, like Munch's 'The Scream', and thought of the jacket of a book she had read, depicting an empty, misty street and a lone child wandering down it with outstretched arms like a somnambulist. Then she recognised an odd, hexagonal building used as a meeting place by some obscure religious sect, and she gave a sob of relief and broke into a run.

Her own front door. That happy sunshine-yellow door with the bare wisteria branches clambering round it, illuminated by an outside light. Another shone from within. Home. But she had left her key behind, and when she rang the bell there was no response, nor did the spaniel bark. She shouted, and banged the knocker, succeeding only in rousing an irate neighbour. Her mother must be at Elliot's. Her mother thought she was safely at Vicky's.

She spent the night in the shed, sleeping fitfully on a pile of garden cushions, conscious of every night-time noise outside, lapsing into tortured dreams from which she awoke with her head aching and mouth bitter-tasting. Gnat was filled with self-pity: she had been outcast from her own house, rejected by her mother whose lover had usurped the daughter's place.

I'll rot here forever. I wish I was dead.

• • •

From the recreation room window Harriet watches the solitary figure standing at the tennis net as though looking out to sea. The figure reminds her of a snail carrying the burden of its house around on its back. Emotion – love, pity, sorrow – blocks her throat and prevents her swallowing. The children, no, not children, have stopped gawping at her and she is struck by the ordinary appearance of most of them, reassured that there are other mothers around who have suffered on account of their progeny; have failed somewhere in their duty of raising them; been defeated. She is touched by the balloons and festivities in her daughter's honour. But the star herself is absent from the celebrations.

'She said she wanted to think,' a gentle boy with a stammer had informed her.

And what *are* her thoughts? Harriet wonders. The mechanisms of her daughters complex mind are unfathomable to her.

She goes into the garden where the wind flattens her skirt against her legs. From her vantage point on the terrace she regards her daughter, immobile by the tennis net. And then the girl turns, and in those protracted seconds while they both stare at each other Harriet sees her daughter's face undergo a series of expressions ranging from incredulity to joy, and is rooted to the spot.

Gnat is disbelieving, convinced Harriet is a figment of her imagination and will disappear. Dizzily she grips the net and shuts her eyes, then re-opens them. Her mother has not moved, is smiling uncertainly as Gnat herself begins to smile uncertainly; and they both start walking slowly towards one another, stopping a couple of feet apart. Harriet's smile becomes tremulous and her chin quivers as she draws close. She can see the remains of smudged tears on her daughter's peaky cheeks, and new ones forming in her eyes. Hers fill also. She lifts Gnat's childish plump hand that always reminded her of a starfish, saying nothing, nor does she embrace her, for fear of rushing things. She massages each finger with its bitten nail in turn, then tenderly enfolds the hand in her own, giving it a little shake of friendship. Gnat clasps it back. She can no longer maintain the smile. Her features have crumpled and tears chase each other into her mouth. Harriet wipes them away. Then, still without speaking, heads inclined towards one another, hands soldered together, they return indoors together.

• • •

Gnat rips open the letter from Dimple with birthday card attached. Her mother had brought it with her.

Dear Gnat,

I wanted to write to you although we had that quarrel (which you started) because, well it is your birthday and everything. I must say I was terribly upset last year when you were so nasty to me, but Mummy said it was because of your father and moving to London, so I forgive you and we can still be friends if you like. Everything's great here. I'm very busy riding and I might be getting a new pony, as the other one doesn't jump well and isn't fast enough. I'm still friends with Camilla and she and I do lots of things together, though I do miss how you and I used to be. What other news? I still like Michael Jackson. I also like Public Enemy. How about you? I've got a new rabbit. He hates the noise of aeroplanes and lets out the weirdest yell whenever he hears one. I hope he gets used to the planes. Have you ever heard a rabbit yell? By the way, I've decided what I'm going to be when I grow up. I'm going to be a beautician. Do you know what you want to be? I can't think of anything else to say. Oh yes, I've got a sort of boyfriend called Ben. His family's terribly rich and important, but I find it a bit yukky kissing him.

See you soon. Don't do anything I wouldn't do.
Love Dimple.

P.S. I'll be having a birthday party soon, so you could come and stay and see my new pony if I have it by then.
P.P.S. I'm enclosing a badge with Kurt Cobain on it for you.

Gnat looks at the card with the pony on it, and reads the letter through twice, quickly and excitedly at first; but then her excitement tones down and changes. As she reads it more thoroughly a slow sense of deflation fills her. The letter seems hollow and unsatisfactory. She pictures Dimple, Dimple with a new pony and a new rabbit and a friend called Camilla; Dimple who is impressed by her sort-of-boyfriend's family; Dimple whose ambition is to be a beautician and who still likes Michael Jackson; who still thinks badges are cool and assumes Gnat does too; who has lagged behind and can never hope to catch up; who would never understand what has happened; who belongs to another life an aeon ago that Gnat cannot recapture.

Very thoughtfully, Gnat replaces the letter, card and badge in the envelope. She does not scrunch it up at all, but lays it carefully in the wastepaper basket, covering it with some other rubbish there, so that no one should think she threw it away accidentally.

She goes over to her cello and takes it from her case and is about to play a piece by Haydn, when she stops. Instead, systematically, she goes through some exercises, over and over again, one after the other, as her old teacher used to make her, her fingers firm and strong and disciplined.

11

'I feel sick,' Gnat groans, leaning forward and clutching her stomach. 'I think I'm going to throw up.'

'It'll be all right. Really it will,' Harriet reassures her.

'I'm going to faint.'

'You're not,' her mother says, holding tight her daughter's hand, on this, their third meeting since Gnat's birthday.

'Don't let go of my hand.'

'I won't.'

After studying the two of them at his leisure, Dr Middleton says, 'Perhaps you would go first, Mrs Edwards.'

The ninth principal event of her adult life.

'We had it all arranged –' she tries to speak evenly, as though about to relate a normal occurrence. 'It was my fortieth birthday and we were going to a restaurant for dinner with Astrid, her boyfriend and another couple. Elliot and I were planning to announce our engagement. We agreed I'd tell Gnat quietly beforehand. I dreaded telling her, but I tried to convince myself she'd be glad.' Harriet gives a short laugh. 'I knew she was fond of him and I thought this might have a stabilising effect on her.'

She breaks off and inhales deeply, like an opera singer preparing for her top note, tries to stop herself from becoming agitated. The quiet young man who looks as though he could be a medical student waits as though he has all the time in the world. He always laces his hands, she notices. Is it deliberate? He urges her on with a slight motion of the head and she clears her throat, not daring to glance at Gnat.

'It was July, early evening . . .'

Warm July. She was wearing her old skimpy dress Oliver had used to love. She had remained painting in the garden as long as possible, postponing the moment, until the nearby church clock chimed half-past six. It could be postponed no longer and, gathering her things, she went inside . . . Heavily up the stairs; reproving herself for being nervous of her own thirteen-year-old child, bottling up anger in advance, thinking that it was absurd she should have to tiptoe cautiously with everything she said for fear of prompting an outburst.

As usual Gnat's door was closed. 'This is MY room' declared the card pinned to it, and beneath the writing was a drawing of the Acid House emblem, like a smiling moon, deceptively merry.

Harriet half opened the door and looked round it: the window open which meant Gnat had been smoking, and the girl was kneeling amongst the mess on the floor, cutting up a black leather skirt she had bought from Oxfam. Harriet walked over to her.

'What are you going to wear tonight?' she asked, by way of broaching the conversation.

'I don't know. I don't think I'll come. I mean it'll be boring with all grown-ups and everything.'

'Of course you must come.'

No reply. Cut, cut.

'Natasha, I want to talk to you. Please put the scissors down for a second.'

'One second,' Gnat said, laying them on the floor, counting, One, and picking them up again.

'Please Natasha, I need to talk. There's something important I want to tell you.'

'Who's stopping you?'

'You make it so hard.'

Crouching down, she attempted to embrace her daughter, who jerked herself away; and Harriet let her arm drop to her side.

The only sound was of Gnat steadily snipping at the skirt with the dressmaking shears, and Harriet felt the anger bubbling to her throat, so that her mouth seemed full. She picked up a piece of leather and toyed with it, kneading its softness. She swallowed back the anger, honeyed her voice. 'Darling, you like Elliot, don't you?'

'I love him. I'm going to marry him,' came the defiant retort.

Dismayed, Harriet didn't know how to go on. Her daughter's ferocious expression, the way she sat tensely upright now, with the shears pointing at her, intimidated her.

There was no alternative. 'Elliot and I – we're engaged,' she said simply in the end.

It happened then, and Harriet re-lives it, sitting beside her daughter in the psychiatrist's room, squeezing her hand.

'I'd had an awful week. I mean a really shitty one,' Gnat says, looking pinched and frightened as she is about to recount the sequence of events she has, until now, blocked from her mind. 'I was feeling really low. Mummy was swanning about with that private smile of hers for days on end, and I knew. I just knew what was going on. And I thought, well, more changes, and where would I come into it all? And I was going crazy with jealousy and all the things going on in my head, and keeping them in. Everything was kind of fighting inside me if you see what I mean. And then Elliot put on this video he'd done a few years ago. It was about Jacqueline du Prè. About her life. And it showed her as a child, and then a girl, playing her cello. And she'd been my heroine. I'd dreamed of being like her. And then it showed her being ill, and she was so brave and everything. And of course she died. It was ever so sad how they did it. I was really creased up seeing that film of her, and watching her play, close-ups of the expression on her face. It really muddled me. I had this great longing to fish out my cello and play it, but I'd cut the strings, so I couldn't. I kept thinking of Daddy, too, because we'd used to listen to that tape of her playing the Elgar together.

'So I went up to my room and lay down. I'd got my face in the pillow so no one would hear me crying. Mummy came in and I pretended to be asleep. I held my breath tight so I wouldn't give the game away, and she touched my hair and left again. I think I half wished she'd stayed. I felt so down and everything. I think I was cross she didn't stay. I heard Elliot and her laughing at something downstairs, and it made me more cross and down than ever. When I got up again and looked at the pillow, it was really funny, as though it was covered with bruises – black from my eye makeup and blue from my lipstick. And then I saw myself in the mirror, and I looked as though I'd been in a punch-up.

'The next day was the last before we broke up from school, and we went on a trip to some pottery in Staffordshire. Anyway, on the way back I saw something that really upset me. I mean it still does.'

A crowd of them on the coach, exuberant after their day's excursion, Walkmen in ears, passing round crisps and sweets. And at the rear, Gnat, along with half a dozen other girls stuck her tongue out and made 'V' signs at the car behind, giggling at the driver's discomfiture. The coach joined the motorway, and within it, the thirty rowdy teenagers swapped jokes and sang, excited at the prospect of breaking up.

And then Gnat saw them: a family of ducks, the mother leading her numerous tiny yellow chicks onto the motorway in a suicide mission. Too late, she realised her error, as one by one they were mown down, and she rushed distractedly to each of her babies in turn, dodging wheels, to try and save it, until she too was run over.

Gnat was inconsolable. She cried all the way back to school, unable to erase from her mind the sight of the mother duck's frantic anguish as she flew between her chicks.

'You eat duck,' reasoned a boy in the row in front.

'I don't. I'm vegetarian.'

'You wear leather shoes.'

'Shut your mouth. Get off her back, will you?' her friend Vicky said. Vicky, who shaved her head at the sides and worked in a supermarket's on a Saturday morning, and cleaned somebody's house two evenings a week; who went to confession and believed in the devil and in Hell; and out of the whole class is the only person Gnat can face.

'So you see, it had been a bad week to start with. And then the day we broke up was Mummy's birthday. In the evening she came into my room when I was cutting up this skirt I'd bought. She was wearing an old dress she'd had for years. It always made me think of our picnics when Daddy was alive, and of Pirate. I knew what she was going to tell me. And inside me I was getting all worked up. It was like years and years of all my feelings inside me were heaping up and frothing, wanting to burst out of me like a volcano. It was this great big mass overtaking me. I mean I couldn't help myself. I couldn't.' Her voice rings out in the quiet of the room.

She turns towards Dr Middleton despairingly, but he gives no indication what he is thinking and she continues.

'I felt all kind of shivery inside me, and I didn't want to

hear what she was going to say. I kept cutting away at the skirt and hoping she'd go away if I did that, and then she asked me if I liked Elliot and I told her I was going to marry him – I thought it would shut her up, and she said—'

'Elliot and I – we're engaged,' Harriet said softly.

The catalyst; followed by the eruption of the volcano. Gnat screaming, 'You can't be, you can't. I won't let you.' Wrestling with her mother, thrusting the sharp dressmaking shears at her. The sweet, skimpy red dress with so many memories attached to it, becoming redder.

Harriet tottered backwards a few steps and stood, swaying slightly, staring at her daughter incredulously.

Gnat dropped the scissors, aghast at what she had done, horrified by the blood spreading over her mother's dress.

'I'm not sorry,' she shouted. 'I'm not sorry. It's all your fault.' And she dashed downstairs where she flung herself onto the hall carpet and hyperventilated.

Harriet crawled to the phone in her room and dialled 999, then made her way to the bathroom. With shaking hands she pulled a towel from the rail and pressed it against herself to staunch the flow of blood. As she lay on the floor trying not to move, gripped with pain, she no longer cared whether she died, because truthfully she couldn't cope with her problems anymore. She heard distant sirens drawing closer, and her daughter downstairs screaming hysterically; her own heartbeat; and had the strangest sensation that this was happening to somebody else and she was observing the scene from afar.

Gnat opened the front door at the sound of the wailing sirens, then sat down. When the two ambulancemen entered they found a young girl hunched in a chair in the hallway, smoking.

'Is it your mother who phoned? Where is she?' one asked.

'Upstairs,' she replied in a flat tone.

'Show us, would you, there's a good girl.'

She led the way, dreading her mother was dead . . .

'I can't go in,' Harriet, lying in the same position, heard her say . . .

And outside the bathroom, Gnat heard her mother's weak voice filtering through: 'I'm all right.'

Gnawing at her nails, she watched them carrying her mother carefully down the stairs, then followed them outside where Harriet was transferred to a stretcher.

'You'd better come with us,' one of the men said to Gnat.

She shook her head vigorously.

'Go to a neighbour's then, there's a good girl.'

The ambulance doors were shut and it was driven off, slowly, then accelerating, the blue light flashing.

On her own she began to hyperventilate again.

Elliot arrived. The front door was ajar and he walked straight in to find her sprawled on the carpet.

She leaped up immediately she saw him and threw herself at him, sobbing, 'I love you, I love you.'

He held her at a distance, seeing the blood speckled on her clothes. 'What's happened? Gnat, where's Mummy?' he demanded.

Terrified by what she had done and what he would think of her, she shrieked, 'I'm not sorry. She made me do it. I'm not sorry.'

'What *are* you on about, Gnat?' Elliot said sharply. And starting for the stairs, he called loudly, 'Harriet, Harriet?'

Gnat tugged at his jacket. 'You can't marry her. I won't let you.'

Ignoring her, he bounded up the stairs, two at a time, with her pursuing him, still hanging onto his jacket.

He was greeted by a trail of blood leading from her bedroom – where on the floor lay the bloodied scissors – to Harriet's, and thence the bathroom; and he leaned

• Valerie Blumenthal

against the wall looking at the red patch on the carpet and the red-stained towels. She saw that he was completely white and his lips had disappeared in his face.

'Where is she? What have you done? What happened?' His voice emerged as a hoarse croak.

She was afraid of his anger and she started shouting once more. If she shouted he couldn't be angry with her. If she shouted, only she could be angry. 'She got hurt with the scissors. They've taken her to hospital. I'm not sorry. I hate her. It's her fault. She made me. I'm not sorry.'

Brushing roughly past her, he ran back downstairs, and looked up a number in Harriet's address book. While he was telephoning Gnat writhed on the hall rug, moaning, 'I can't breathe. I can't breathe.' Her face started to swell.

The doctor arrived. He knew Gnat. He knew Harriet better, from all those occasions she had visited him in despair. By now Gnat was screaming, her features distorted beyond recognition, and he quickly assessed the situation and himself made a telephone call.

She was dimly aware of Elliot trying to pinion her hands to prevent her scratching at her inflamed body, of his soothing tones infiltrating her frenzy; the doorbell ringing.

The doctor answered it. 'Good of you to come so promptly.'

There were two of them, a man and a woman. She knows now that the man was a consultant adolescent psychiatrist and the woman a social worker. She remembers muffled speaking; her itching, burning body; not being able to breathe; her numb nose and mouth. She does not remember the injection which sedated her; and what ensued is hazy: someone kneeling over her, a single eye boring into hers, a cool flannel on her forehead. And another siren. Being carried into an ambulance. Then she must have slept, because the next thing she knew was that she was being assisted to her feet. She was at Turner's End.

* * *

Gnat stops talking. The room seems to have magnified out of all proportion. The echoes of her dying tones still reverberate. She cannot bring herself to look at her mother or Dr Middleton. Her cheeks bear red imprints from the pressure of her fingers, and one of her nails is bleeding round the cuticle from her chewing it. And without warning she vomits onto the floor. Her mother supports her as she retches. At last there is nothing left, and she stands there staring at the fetid pool.

'I'm sorry,' she whispers to Harriet. 'I'm sorry,' she sobs. 'Sorry, sorry, sorry. I'm sorry for what I did.'

• • •

'Gnat, how do you feel about going home on Friday?'

'Home? You mean properly home, or just for the weekend?' she asks, trying to sound calm.

'Properly home.'

She is overcome by a tide of emotions. She wants to laugh and laugh, and cry and cry. She just sits there immobile.

'Gnat?'

A thought occurs to her. 'Does she know? What does Mummy say?'

He puts on his I'm-going-to-be-straight-with-you-expression and a small chill runs through her.

'She's glad, but she is also anxious.'

'Oh.' She swallows on her disappointment. 'I thought she liked me now.'

'She does.'

'But she doesn't want me back.' Her pixie, crestfallen face looks everywhere but at him.

'I did not say that. Gnat, you really must try not to put a false interpretation on remarks.'

'But you said—'

'I said she was anxious. That does not mean she doesn't want you back. It means just that: she is anxious. She's

• Valerie Blumenthal

being realistic that's all. And so must you be. There's no point in pretending a situation can go from being bad to good so easily. Things don't happen like that.'

'Oh. You mean she doesn't trust me.' She tries to control the rapid quivering of her chin which heralds a cascade of tears.

'Would you expect her to?'

She lets her head sag onto her chest and lifts the neck of her jumper up to cover her chin and mouth. 'No.'

'If you were her, would you trust you?'

'No.'

'Well then.'

They've started. The tears. Within the cave of her jumper she blots them with the woolly fabric. Compassionately he watches her heaving shoulders.

'It's up to you, Gnat,' he says to her shrouded head.

A brightening; a little bright feeling inside her.

'What I'm saying is you mustn't expect too much from each other. If you are going to be unrealistic in your expectations, then you will be disappointed and let down. Do you understand what I'm saying?'

'Yes . . . So I'm on trial?' Her voice is distorted through her jumper.

'No more than your mother is on trial with you.'

'But *I* could be shoved back in here any time, couldn't I?'

'Yes, but I doubt you would be.'

'Oh God I can't stand it.'

'Yes you can. And I think things will work out if you're sensible. Your mother loves you very much. She wants it to work. She's going to do her utmost to see that it does.'

'Has she said that?' She wriggles up straight again and releases her jumper. Her face is tear-drenched.

'Yes she has.'

'Honestly?'

'I've never lied to you, Gnat.'

She goes up to her room. There are three days left, but

she starts doing things in readiness, to make it sink in: takes down her posters, peels off the blu-tak and rolls them up, puts them in her case. Folds up some of her underwear and puts it in there, leaving three spare pairs of knickers and a clean bra in the chest of drawers. And faster and faster she packs, books, cards, makeup, clothes, all going into the case.

I'm going home. I'm going home. I'm going home, she tells herself, trying to make it sink in.

'You're going home,' states Maria, who has been standing for some minutes in the doorway, unnoticed.

Gnat looks up from her frenetic activity and the two girls confront each other very seriously.

'Yes.'

Maria shrugs and attempts a smile but her lovely face puckers.

Gnat goes up to her and the two girls rock there on the spot in a deep embrace.

'You'll be getting out one day, too,' says Gnat when they've pulled away from each other.

'Oh yeah. Then where?' asks poor, tormented Maria.

• • •

Dear Mrs Edwards,

It was a pleasure to see you yesterday, and I am glad that your day's outing with Gnat was so fruitful.

With regard to your daughter's homecoming this weekend, I thought I would write to 'put you in the picture', so to speak. As I mentioned, it is customary for patients to spend weekends with their families by way of gradual rehabilitation, before returning on a permanent basis; however, every case must be judged on its own merit and in Gnat's instance I believe this could be counter-productive and unsettling. I believe that the time is right for her to try to enrol in normal life again.

You have seen for yourself the progress Gnat has made since she has been here, and she has shown herself to be a girl of honesty and courage besides possessing intelligence, sharp wit and musical talent. However, she is highly-strung and still prone to vacillating moods of depression and elation, and to fits of temper which prevent her from reasoning logically. Given time and nurturing she should learn to manage, if not conquer, these aspects of her nature and to integrate more easily in society. Already, in the relatively short time she has been here there has been a marked improvement. You will need to be firm as well as loving towards her, and it will certainly not all be plain sailing. Those characteristics of your daughter which are her strengths – determination, wilfulness and single-mindedness – are also her weaknesses. There will be times when you will feel bewildered and frustrated and close to giving up. There are many years to be recovered, and things do not happen overnight.

With regard to the immediate future: as we discussed, I would suggest Gnat move to another school as soon as possible, somewhere fairly small with a sensitive approach to young people and a good academic standard, without a competitive environment. There is one in particular I can recommend, not too distant from you. Meanwhile, you may find that initially Gnat clings to you and seems rather lost. Patience.

As I told both of you yesterday, I would strongly advise that you and she continue with joint therapy for several months at least, and would be pleased to assist you in arranging this. I know someone convenient for where you live who will be sympathetic to your situation. Of course, I am always at the other end of the telephone if you need me, and enclose my home number.

And now we must keep our fingers crossed for the future. I reiterate that word, patience.

With kind regards,

Roger Middleton.

• • •

Tom's workshop is a hive of activity. Radio 2 is playing and the kettle boiling, while Tom saws away at a piece of wood. He glances up when she comes in.

'Who's in time for a cup of tea then?'

She makes it, brings over their mugs and sits by him on the bench.

'Just what I needed,' he says, lifting the mug to his lips

unsteadily. He mops up the spilled drops of tea with a crumpled yellowed handkerchief. 'Arthritis. I shan't be able to go on working much longer.'

'Will that make you sad?'

'I daresay. To begin with. But there'll be other things to do. Everything has its time. We all have our time. Talking about that, I haven't seen you for ages. And you've had your birthday. What have you been up to then?'

'I'm going home, Tom.'

He studies her bright face and his own creases into a gap-toothed grin.

'Well I never. Well that's good news then, isn't it? I'll miss seeing you though. Miss your chatter – and the tea of course. Cheers an old man up it does, to have young company.'

'I'll come and visit you.'

'Nah. Of course you won't. Forget all about old Tom you will.'

'I shan't,' she protests.

'And it's right you should,' he says, pointing a misshapen finger at her; 'Got to get on with your life proper now. Put this behind you.'

He gets up and goes over to another part of the workshop, returns carrying something.

'Here, I made you this for your birthday.' He passes her the box and she stares at it.

'For me?'

'Yes.'

'It's really lovely.' She strokes the different inlaid woods, the small brass escutcheon, and tries the key. Inside the box is a lift-out compartmented tray. Tom watches her as she closes and opens the lid again.

'Thank you so much,' she says shyly. 'I mean I really love it. I can keep private things in it.'

'Anything you like. A secret treasure trove. Here – I wanted to write a note to put inside, but my spelling's not up to much, and I wasn't sure about how to spell your name again.'

He takes a sheet of paper from a notepad and reaches for the pencil he keeps tucked behind his right ear.

'How do you spell your name then?'

'Gnat with a G. G-N-A-T.'

He licks the pencil and writes painstakingly in child-like script, 'To Gnat, with best wishes for the futer from yor freand Tom.'

Her eyes cloud over.

'Here, you're never crying.'

She shakes her head, trying to smile.

'That's all right then. Silly mite.'

She finishes her tea. Time to go. Her mother will be arriving. She hugs him, wrapping her arms tight around him, feeling his hard, stubbly cheek against hers, and then leaves. Tom appears at the window, just as he was when she first saw him; tanned face wreathed in smiles, his hair a shock of white. They wave to each other. She feels as though she has a fish bone stuck in her throat, and her eyes smart.

Gnat starts walking back to Turner's End, thinking: that it will be the last time she does this walk; that it hasn't all been bad; imagining how it will be when she goes home; the house with the yellow front door; her own bedroom with the patchwork quilt and all her bits round the mirror; ordinary things like cleaning out Rodent Mark 2's cage, and playing her cello, and Sundays.

• • •

Harriet has bought a giant bear with a tartan bow at its neck and propped it against the pillows of Gnat's bed. Downstairs, balloons bob from the hall ceiling; there are vases of flowers everywhere. The fridge is stocked with satay sauce and chocolate spread, and the freezer with Mars ice-creams.

She has hardly slept for two nights, has lain pressed into the firm 'S' of Elliot's body, awake as though she has drunk a hundred cups of coffee, awake with her fluctuating emotions: happiness, excitement, apprehension; one minute optimistic, the next fearful of all the things that could go wrong, a repetition of the quarrels and defiance and shrieking. The house has at least been peaceful for the past couple of months. She watches the different stages of night cast the bedroom in a progression of patterns and lights and shadows. Even in his sleep, Elliot's arm is protective around her.

Lucky. Yes, I'm lucky.

And now Harriet closes the yellow front door behind her, climbs into the car, and drives off to Turner's End; to bring her daughter home.

The tenth principal event of her adult life.